GHOST AND FOUND

A REAPER WITCH MYSTERY

ELLE ADAMS

To be notified when Elle Adams's next book is released, sign up to her author newsletter.

1

Ghosts really did have the worst sense of timing. I was on my way to a date with Drew Gardener when the spirit of a young man began to follow me down the darkening road. The ghost wore a mournful expression that put me in mind of a lost puppy, which might have worked if I hadn't seen it a million times before.

Running into these situations was inevitable in a town like Hawkwood Hollow, which contained more ghosts than living people, but I was supposed to be going on a date, not running errands for spirits. With the short skirt and heeled boots I'd picked to wear, I wouldn't be doing much running anyway.

When the ghost inevitably floated directly into my path, I sidestepped him. "I'm a little busy here."

"I need your help," the ghost said, undeterred. "Can you please take a message to my wife? I've been waiting forever for someone to finally see me."

"How long have you been waiting, exactly?"

"Seven years."

"Then you can wait a little longer." Unfair, maybe, but this was my first shot at a serious date with the detective in weeks, and I refused to let anyone derail me, living or dead.

"I can offer you something in return." He drifted along behind me. "I can help you get where you're going."

"No thanks."

I'd never been to the shifters' part of town before, but asking for directions from a lost spirit was a great way to end up at the bottom of the river. I'd barely managed to shake off the ghost of my twin brother, Mart, whose annoying habit of offering a constant commentary on my decisions was not something I wanted in my dating life. Considering it'd been a long time since I'd *had* a dating life, and Drew couldn't see ghosts himself, he didn't need to endure me spending the evening conversing with the dead.

In any case, my rejection worked. The ghost sadly drifted away, while I turned left down the darkening street and kept both eyes open for the park that marked the boundary of the shifters' part of town. Drew had texted me directions, but there was a surprising lack of working street lamps in this part of town, and someone had helpfully removed all the nearby road signs. A moon-drunk werewolf, maybe. Thick bushes bordered the roads, and patches of woodland filled the spaces between houses, providing plenty of room for young shifters to run and for older shifters to blow off steam.

Since werewolves lost their clothes when they shifted, it was probably better for all of us that they had some semblance of cover, but the result was that the park was awash in darkness as pitch-black as the afterworld. The signpost marking the park's entrance loomed ahead of me, but it was too dark to read the words imprinted on it. I pulled out my phone and checked Drew's message. He'd told me to meet him at the east entrance, but it was beyond me to figure out if this was the right one. The park had at least a dozen ways in and out, and that was if you discounted the fences that most werewolves simply climbed over anyway. Tricky.

I waited for five minutes before entering the park and following the path around the exterior, figuring that as long as I stuck to the right side of the park, I was bound to run into Drew at some point. Dense bushes bordered the path to either side of me, and each small noise made me tense up. Ghosts I could deal with, but I wasn't sure non-shifters were strictly welcome in this park, and werewolves were generally the strike-first-ask-questions-later type.

As I reached the next entrance, a head popped up out of the bushes, making me jump. Instinctively, I reached for my Reaper powers, shadows filling my hands. That had the unfortunate side effect of making the darkness even more absolute, and consequently, I hadn't taken more than a step before I tripped, my heeled boots sending me headfirst into the bushes and on top of the intruder who'd given me such a fright.

Not a ghost but a living person, who yelped, "Mercy!"

I disentangled myself from the stranger and stumbled out of the bushes, willing the shadows to subside. "Sorry, you startled me."

A young woman straightened upright, clutching a pair

of what appeared to be binoculars. "I'm Belinda Jennings. I was stargazing."

"In the shifters' park?"

She didn't look like a werewolf. Short and slight, she wore her dark hair in pigtails, which made her look barely out of her teens, if that.

"Yes, the stars are very bright from here. Look." She held out her binoculars in demonstration.

Nonplussed, I found that the lenses were covered in some kind of dark fabric dotted with white splotches, like a child's drawing of the night sky. In the real world, the trees were too thick and the clouds too dense to see the stars or moon, but I was at a loss as to whether she could see anything through the binoculars either.

"I'll take your word for it." I handed them back. "Might want to look a bit closer to Earth in future in case anyone else trips over you."

"I saw you coming, you know."

Okay... "Can you actually see through those things?"

"Oh, not with my eyes." She gave a high-pitched laugh. "I saw the future. I knew you were going to walk into me almost a minute before you did."

"Wouldn't you have known I was coming anyway, if you were looking in my direction instead of at the sky?" I'd never had much patience with people who claimed to see the future, magical or not, and if she was a genuine Seer, I was a unicorn. On the other hand... "I don't suppose you've seen a werewolf on the path in the last few minutes?"

"Yes, lots of them," she said. "There are always werewolves in here."

Probably because you're standing in their park. She wasn't a shifter herself, since most Seers were witches, but I doubted she could see further than the end of her nose, and even that was debatable, considering those binoculars of hers.

"I meant specifically on this path and within the last five minutes. Or ten." Drew was a little late, but it was entirely possible I'd picked the wrong entrance, and he was on the other side of the park. "I'm supposed to be meeting someone here."

"Oh, don't do that," she said. "This isn't the place to be. There is an ill omen in the air. Can't you sense it?"

All right. I'd had about enough of listening to her nonsense. "Believe me, I don't plan on sticking around."

I left her standing in the bushes and walked the rest of the way to the next entrance. There, to my relief, I spotted Drew waiting on the other side of the path, concealed from sight by the shadow of a large tree.

"There you are." I trekked towards him. "Next time, I think we should pick a meeting place with more lights."

"Hey." The blond werewolf's handsome face was a welcome sight, and so was the kiss he planted on my cheek when I caught him up. "I didn't think it was that confusing to navigate."

"Not all of us have great night vision."

He raised a brow. "I thought that'd be an advantage for a Reaper."

"I can navigate my own shadows just fine, but they generally don't have werewolves lurking in them."

"I'd hope not."

Joking aside, I'd been starting to worry that I'd picked

the wrong route altogether and unintentionally trespassed on the ground of one of the notoriously territorial factions of the local werewolf pack. Drew had seemed insistent that not being a werewolf meant I wouldn't be at risk of that, but being jumped by a pack of wolves was not how I wanted to spend my date night.

"I'll keep that in mind in future," he said. "So… are you ready to meet some of the locals?"

"Erm…" I hoped so, but I was always wary of meeting new paranormals who'd only heard of me by reputation alone. And boy, did I have one. "Provided no ghosts show up, yes."

"That's unlikely," he said. "Most shifters can't see ghosts, so I can't imagine they'd get much entertainment over here."

"True," I acknowledged. "I met one on the way here, but I sent him packing."

"And your brother?"

"He stayed behind."

"Good," he said. "I'd rather keep this date between the two of us."

My heart flipped over, and then my ears pricked up when rustling came from the nearby bushes. Noticing too, Drew followed Belinda Jennings's progress as she waded through the bushes as if there wasn't a perfectly serviceable footpath nearby. "Who's that?"

"I ran into her on the way in," I replied in an undertone. "She said she's stargazing and that she can see into the future."

Drew watched her trip over a bramble and fall into a tangled heap. "Looks like she's having trouble seeing into the present."

"You aren't wrong, but I tripped over her in the bushes while looking for you."

"Maybe I should wear a flashing light on my head next time. Or carry a sign with your name on it."

"Oi, watch it, you." I grinned despite myself, falling into the same easy banter which came naturally between the two of us. "My eyesight isn't that bad. At least I'm not trying to see the night sky through a pair of binoculars with the lenses covered."

"That's what she's doing?" He laughed under his breath. "Maura, I don't think you need to run into ghosts to attract trouble. You find weirdos without even trying."

"Ha ha."

Talking to Drew was easy enough that I sometimes forgot how relatively recently we'd met. In fact, we hadn't exactly given one another the best of first impressions, since I'd been trying to evacuate an unwanted ghost from an old house and he'd been the detective investigating the ghost's death. Naturally, he'd thought I was a trouble-maker, which wasn't precisely wrong, but we'd managed to reconcile our differences, and here we were.

"How's work?" he asked.

"Good," I said. "Busy as usual, but we have another potential staff member coming for a trial tomorrow, and Allie seems pretty confident that this one'll stick."

"I hope she's right."

I had to admit I wasn't feeling her optimism. Our last bartender had gone to jail for murder, and we'd had trouble finding a replacement, partly because I'd also ticked off the local witch coven when I'd driven their former leader out of town for attempting to cover up the murders in question. As a result, a good portion of the town's witches wanted nothing to do with me out of principle, and we'd been left with a grand total of three staff members to work at the inn's restaurant, one of whom was a fifteen-year-old who was at school most of the time.

Really, it was no wonder that I'd had precious few hours to set aside for dating the town's chief of police, who had a busy enough schedule of his own.

"So how's the pack?" I asked in an attempt to change the subject. "Still trying your patience?"

"That's one way of putting it," he said. "The pack is divided into several factions, and I can guarantee that at least two of them are arguing at any given time. Things have been a little tense lately, since the pack chief's youngest daughter was supposed to be marrying the son of a former rival this weekend. I say *supposed to* because she got cold feet at the last minute, and now she says she's not going through with it."

"Fun." Frankly, I'd rather deal with the combined trouble of the local ghosts and an angry witch coven than navigate werewolf drama. I hadn't had much experience with shifters, but this was the longest I'd spent in a single town since I'd ditched my Reaper apprenticeship following my twin brother's untimely death.

Since then, I'd drifted around from one town to another, some paranormal and some not. Being partway between a witch and a Reaper meant I tended to be the odd duck in most scenarios, and even moving to Hawkwood Hollow hadn't exactly been smooth sailing, considering that I'd already burned bridges with the local coven and that the one other Reaper in town was not my biggest fan. The shifters had no reason to dislike me, though… right?

As we left the park, a commotion rose up from somewhere among the trees. A chorus of shouts and growls ripped through the night, and the detective's steps halted. "I think there's trouble."

"Sounds that way to me."

It also sounded like a situation I didn't want to involve myself in, but standing alone in the darkness didn't appeal either, so I kept close behind Drew as he walked towards the source of the noise.

In a clearing, several shifters had gathered around something lying on the grass. My heart lurched when one of them shone a light onto the body of a man with broad shoulders and dark blond hair, who lay unmoving on his back, his clothes smeared with mud.

"What's going on here?" Drew's voice cut through the clamour.

"That's Davey Rogers," one of the nearby werewolves growled. "Someone killed him and hid his body in the bushes."

"Nobody comes in here but the pack," said another. "We have a killer in our midst."

"Was he wounded? Let me see." Drew moved towards the body, but two of the werewolves barred his path, their suspicious gazes landing on me. Oh no.

"Who's she?" a burly werewolf demanded. "What's she doing here?"

"Maura's been with me the whole time she was here," Drew said.

I hadn't, technically, but I certainly hadn't seen a body when I'd been stumbling around the bushes. I hoped

Belinda had had the sense to move away from here before she got implicated in the werewolf's murder.

Murder. How did I always walk into these situations?

"Who found him?" Drew asked. "Tell me everything."

"I saw his foot sticking out of the bushes," said the burly werewolf. "I recognised him at once. Davey's supposed to be marrying the chief's daughter this weekend. Who did this to him?"

"If I had to guess," growled another werewolf, "I'd say it was someone from *your* faction of the pack. You wanted to stop the wedding, and you got your wish."

His words set off a crescendo of horrible ripping noises as the burly werewolf shifted into animal form, shedding his clothes in the process. Seconds later, two huge, furred wolves with sharp teeth squared up to one another, surrounded by a chorus of growls.

Drew moved in front of me. "Maura, I'd take cover. They're angry, and unstable shifters can't always distinguish between friend and foe."

Since I was a long way from being their friend, that would get me put firmly in the *foe* category. I got the message and backed away, tripping over Belinda Jennings for the second time that night. "Ow. Sorry."

She lowered her binoculars. "You're back. I knew you would be."

"I never left." I really didn't want to hear any more nonsense from her, but with several angry werewolves standing a few metres away, I'd have to stay put for now. "When you told me there was an ill omen, is this what you meant?"

"Oh, no," she said. "It's not the full moon yet, you see."

There didn't need to be a full moon for shifters to

revert to their animal forms and start brawling, and it took less than a high-profile murder for them to come to blows.

On the other hand, while Belinda's binoculars meant she was more likely to have seen the ground up close than the murderer, I couldn't resist trying a question. "Did you see the man who died?"

A loud growl drowned out the end of my question. I whipped my head around, seeing that Drew had moved to position himself between the two werewolves but had remained in human form. Worry clenched inside my chest even though I knew that he was capable of shifting into a werewolf himself if necessary, and I fought the urge to drag him into the shadows of the afterworld and out of harm's way.

Belinda caught my arm, making me jump so violently I almost gave away my location. "Can you not do that?" I hissed.

"My apologies," she said. "Look, they're shifting back."

Sure enough, the werewolves turned from furred beasts into naked humans, and I averted my gaze. Typically, Drew hadn't shifted, so his clothes were a hundred percent intact. What was with my luck tonight?

Belinda continued to stare at me, as if there weren't a half-dozen extremely nude werewolves standing next to our hiding place. "You talk with the dead, don't you?"

"When they let me get a word in edgeways." It was no big secret that I could see ghosts, and besides, maybe she'd seen me talking to the spirit who'd tailed me earlier. "Why?"

"You hear things nobody else does. Like me."

"Trust me, you don't want to hear what most ghosts

have to say." Since the shifters were no longer growling and furred, I deduced that they weren't going to attack Drew, so I made my careful way through the bushes and back to the path.

By the time I'd found the entrance again, Drew caught up to me. "I'm sorry, Maura, but it'll be safer if you go home. I'm going to have to clear up this mess, or else it'll get even more unpleasant than it already is."

"It's fine," I said, except it wasn't. Someone was dead, and the werewolves might well try to tear one another to pieces again while I was gone. If they did, Drew would be obligated to intervene, being both a pack member and the head of the local law enforcement. Yes, it was his job, but I'd hoped our night would end with a kiss, not potential bodily harm.

"I'll message you later." He disappeared into the bushes, while I watched him leave, wishing there was more I could do to help. Yet my only area of expertise was talking to spirits, and while the victim's ghost might show up at some point to clear up matters, there was usually a delay of at least a day between when someone died and when their ghost appeared. I definitely did not want to stick around until then, so I found myself heading home alone.

To no surprise whatsoever, the ghost of the young man who'd accosted me earlier reappeared as I left the park behind.

"You're back," he said. "Can you help me? Please?"

Sensing he'd probably follow me back to the inn if I refused, I came to a resigned halt. "What do you want me to do for you, then?"

"I need to tell my wife that I'm sorry I ate the last cookie."

"You think she'll remember after seven years?" In response, he just gave me that sad neglected puppy look, and I caved in. "Fine, fine, I'll tell her."

Don't let any ghosts tell you that I'm not helpful when I want to be.

2

———

"Rise and shine!" Mart sang loudly, rousing me from sleep. "It's a beautiful day."

I grunted. "If you say so."

I shielded my eyes against the sunlight, while my twin brother floated around the room, humming to himself. Being a ghost, he hadn't been able to do much more than make the curtains flutter, but I'd have preferred to lie in bed for a bit longer rather than get up and have to tell Carey about yesterday's disastrous end.

"What's got you in such a bad mood today?" he said. "Was your date a bust?"

"It never happened."

Mart had been sulking somewhere when I'd returned to the inn because he'd taken offence at my demand that he leave Drew and me alone for our date, so I hadn't told him the details yet.

"What do you mean, it didn't?" he said. "You got all dressed up and everything."

"Way to rub it in my face, Mart."

"How was I supposed to know?" he said indignantly. "Why'd you come back so late, then?"

"A ghost talked me into passing on a message to his wife."

"Aww," he said. "That's sweet. So what made the detective change his mind?"

"Someone got murdered in the park." I climbed out of bed. "A werewolf."

"Murdered?" His brow shot up. "Was he the one whose ghost you had to run errands for?"

"No, his ghost won't have appeared yet," I reminded him. "Granted, it'd be helpful if it did, because the werewolves were about to tear one another to shreds yesterday."

"Uh-oh," he said. "Did Drew have to shift and talk them down?"

"Nah, he stayed in human form." I pushed the bedcovers back into place. "I got to look at far more naked werewolves than I ever intended to, but at least nobody ripped one another's heads off."

Mart snorted. "Guess you only wanted to see one naked werewolf, not several."

I'd walked right into that one. "I'd settle for a date which isn't interrupted by either a dead body or a ghost. Anyway, I left before things got hairy again. Literally."

Leaving Mart laughing behind me, I went to shower before checking my phone for any texts from Drew. Nothing. Worry fluttered inside me, though no news wasn't necessarily bad news. I fired off a quick message asking if he was okay and got ready for my shift at the inn.

As I worked full time at the Riverside Inn, Allie had let

me pick out a room for my own, one of many perks to the job. It was nice not to stress about dealing with angry landlords over the nonsense Mart did like accidentally flooding the bathroom due to his inexplicable liking for hot showers.

While the furniture in the room was fairly basic, I didn't need anything more. My possessions were minimal, a necessity when I'd spent years moving from place to place, and it'd taken me weeks to do the simple task of transferring my clothes from my suitcase to the wardrobe. Including my one nice outfit. I suppressed a sigh, not knowing when Drew and I would have the chance to resume our date, before leaving the room.

I went downstairs to grab breakfast before the new potential bartender showed up for her trial shift. To say I was a little apprehensive was an understatement, given that the last few trials had all been unequivocal disasters. I smiled at Allie when I spotted her behind the desk in the lobby. Allie Forbes had long, dark hair streaked with grey, and she wore a maroon cloak and a matching pointed hat today.

"Is the trial going ahead? She's coming after Carey goes to school, right?"

"Yes," she replied. "She might be a little early, as she's flying in from out of town."

"Oh?" I raised a brow. "Is that why she said yes?"

If she didn't know my reputation, no wonder she'd readily agreed to come.

"Actually, she used to live here," said Carey's mother. "She left town over a disagreement with Mina."

I nodded in understanding. "So you told her the coast is clear now that Mina's gone?"

"Pretty much," she said. "She agreed to come back for a trial run, since she's looking for a new job anyway, so she's not likely to back out."

"Hope you're right."

Her words gave my mood a boost, since anyone who'd challenged Mina Devlin was someone I wouldn't mind as a co-worker. The manipulative ex-coven leader had held the town under her grip since before the flood which had struck the town two decades prior, causing the river to overflow its banks and kicking off an infestation of ghosts, which continued to this day.

Very few people were aware that the flood itself might be among the many misdeeds that Mina Devlin had covered up, given that all evidence of its cause had literally washed away. In fact, only myself and the town's retired Reaper knew some of the truth, and there were gaping holes in our knowledge. For that reason, old Harold had refused point-blank to make an accusation against the coven. Since nobody actually knew where Mina Devlin had fled to, we wouldn't get very far by trying to report her crimes.

I shoved all thoughts of Mina firmly out of mind, while I walked through the automatic doors connecting the reception to the restaurant which stood adjacent to the inn. I loaded a plate from the buffet table and joined Carey at a table near the bar. She wore her usual yellow-and-white school uniform with her bright-red ghost goggles sitting on the table next to her laptop.

Her black cat, Casper, had curled up on her lap, occasionally sticking his paw into a bowl of milk and licking it.

"Hey, Maura." She looked up and beamed at me. "How was your date?"

I groaned inwardly. "Didn't happen. Something urgent with the pack came up, and since Drew is the chief of police, he had to deal with it. We'll reschedule for later."

"That's a shame." The corners of her mouth turned down. "I know you were looking forward to it."

I checked my phone. Drew hadn't messaged me back yet, but he might be asleep. It must have been a late night for him, so I tried not to dwell on it. "How's the blog?"

"Great." She brightened. "I'll need some more footage soon, though, and I wondered if we might try somewhere outside of town next time."

"Like where?" I didn't necessarily share Carey's passion for finding haunted properties and filming their inhabitants, but my own penchant for attracting ghosts had served us both well in helping her gain footage to share online. It was Carey who'd brought me here to Hawkwood Hollow to begin with, in fact, and since she and her mother had given me my first stable job in a long time, I owed her.

"I've been researching." She indicated her laptop. "I'm looking at magical communities with known resident ghosts or unsolved cases which seem to point to ghostly involvement. I think it'll boost my audience to be able to give some variety."

"If you want to go stay in another town, you're going to need permission from your mum."

"She'll go with us, of course. We can do a weekend trip."

"Can she leave the inn for that long?" I asked.

"If our new bartender turns out to be good enough, then I don't see why not."

"Might be getting ahead of yourself there, but it's nice to imagine."

Carey's relentless optimism was pretty much the polar opposite of my usual attitude, so I had to be careful not to rain on her parade. I doubted Allie would entrust anyone else with managing the inn in her absence, which meant that I'd probably have to take on sole responsibility for Carey myself. If I were Allie, I'd be sceptical of my ability to keep both of us out of trouble, given my past record.

Despite all that, I'd been enjoying helping with Carey's ghost-hunting ventures. I'd once been training to be a Reaper, and while I'd left that life behind, I'd always felt vaguely guilty about not doing enough to help the ghosts I saw on a regular basis. This way was decidedly better than my previous job at the morgue, from which I'd got fired for sharing the local ghosts' funeral plans with their non-deceased relatives.

Soon enough, Carey left for school, while I went behind the bar to wait for the arrival of the new potential bartender. A short Asian girl with shoulder-length dark hair strode in a minute later, dressed in plain black trousers and a T-shirt depicting a cat with the caption "We're all mad here." She'd showed up ten minutes early, which in my estimation automatically put her above several of the other people we'd trialled.

"Hey." She bounded over to the bar. "I take it you're Maura?"

"That's me. You're here for the trial?"

"I'm Jia." She peered behind the counter. "Are Allie and Carey around?"

"Carey just went to school," I said. "Allie is working at reception, but I can give you a quick tour of the place before we get too busy."

I started off by handing her an apron to wear for the duration of her trial before showing her the kitchens and the area behind the bar. She'd clearly worked in this kind of environment before, so I didn't have to do too much hand-holding. Clearing away the breakfast supplies was much faster with two of us. While she waved her wand to levitate a stack of plates into the kitchen, she cast a glance in my direction. "So I hear you drove Mina out of town."

I managed to refrain from dropping the pile of glasses I was levitating—barely. "Did Allie tell you?"

A smile played on her mouth. "She told me a little, but I wanted to hear it from the perspective of the person who drove her away."

I finished levitating the glasses to safety before answering. "Mina turned out to be covering up for a murderer, which is also how we ended up with a vacancy here. Our last bartender was the culprit."

"Lucky you came here when you did, then."

"Not for Mina."

She gave a laugh. "True that. I always hoped someone would put her away, but she's slipperier than a greased broomstick."

You're telling me. Did she know the extent of the former coven leader's crimes, though? "Nobody knows where she ran off to."

"She'll have gone to one of her bolt holes," she said. "She has friends and connections in high places, but she's also on the run. Now would be the ideal time to corner her, I reckon."

"I don't know anything about her hiding places," I replied. "I also don't exactly have clout. I'm not part of a coven, and I never have been."

"Fair enough." I detected some disappointment in her tone. Maybe she'd hoped I was willing to join forces and bring Mina to justice.

The idea did hold some appeal, I had to admit. Mina certainly deserved jail time, but the magical world was an insular one and was also spread out across countless small communities, which meant tracking down one individual was difficult even if you didn't take magic into account. With the number of magical means of hiding one's identity, it'd take a lot of persistence to make her resurface. She might even have left the country, for all we knew.

I waved my wand and cast a cleaning spell on the crockery stacked on the work surface in the kitchen. "What did the two of you argue about?"

"What didn't we argue about?" She helped me clean up the crockery before returning to the bar. "My dad died when I was a kid, and my mum and I moved here. Mina was all smiles at first, happy to let us join the coven. Provided we followed her rules, that is."

I waited for a moment for her to continue. "I'm guessing you didn't?"

She shrugged. "The other kids at school treated me like an outsider. Since some of them were related to other high-up members of the coven, Mina wouldn't hear a word against them. She and my mum had a blazing argument. I don't know all the details, but my mum came straight back home and said we were leaving town. I didn't want to, and I managed to convince her to stay for a few years, but Mum didn't dare stand up to Mina again."

"That's awful."

"After I graduated from the academy, I stuck around for a few years just to spite her," added Jia. "My mum moved away, but I tried to get my foot in the door with the coven. I hoped I'd be able to bring about some change from within, but Mina barred me at every turn. My own magic was never great, so I had no way to challenge her. Eventually, I left for good, and I gave up on the idea of coming back here for a long while. When I heard someone drove her out of town, though, I had to come back and see what it was all about."

"Honestly, it was partly an accident," I admitted. "The rest of the coven practically hero-worshipped her, though, which made it a bit hard to find any willing replacements to work here."

"I bet," she said. "We're better off without any of those sycophants. I'm much more fun to work with."

Jia struck me as the kind of person who spoke her mind, while Mina had preferred everyone to support her decisions and hated dissent. It was no wonder they'd come into conflict, though I had to wonder how many others had been treated the same as Jia.

"Driving off coven leaders is not something I do on a regular basis," I told her. "My thing is usually handling ghosts."

"Oh, Allie told me about that too." Her expression brightened. "You're a ghost hunter?"

"I don't hunt ghosts. It's usually the other way around." If Allie had told her, did Jia know I was a Reaper too? Carey was obsessed with ghosts despite her own lack of skill at seeing spirits, but the instant Mart showed his face, I wouldn't be able to keep it quiet.

"The ghosts hunt you?" She snorted. "I can see why Carey's blog is gaining traction."

"Do you read it?" I asked. "If so, please tell Carey. You'll make her whole week."

"Speaking of ghosts." Her gaze went to the door where Mart had just floated into view, and she followed his progress across the restaurant. *She can see him?*

"That's my brother, Mart, the inn's resident ghost. I didn't know you could see them too."

"She can?" Mart leapt behind the counter and danced in triumph. "At last! I was starting to think I'd be stuck with your company alone forever."

"Huh." Jia's brow furrowed. "Maura, how'd your brother end up haunting the inn?"

"He's not haunting the inn, he's haunting me."

"I'm haunting her," he agreed.

She looked between us in bemusement. This would take some getting used to, since most people could only hear one side of my conversations with ghosts.

"I can see why you wanted to start running ghost tours at the inn," she said.

"Allie told you that too?" I guessed. "We have more than one resident ghost. You must have seen the others."

"Yeah, that was one of the other reasons I wasn't sorry to leave town," she said. "Not that the ghosts are that scary, but it's always weird being able to see people that nobody else can."

"Some of them are scary," Mart put in. "Some of us are delightful."

"In your dreams."

"Mart, do you help out at the bar?" she asked. "I've never met a ghostly bartender before."

He pouted. "I try, but she won't let me do anything important."

"Because you can turn the tap on but can't turn it off again," I pointed out. "Don't look at me like that. You know it's true. You flooded the kitchen when I put you on dishwashing duty."

"There might be other things he can do." Jia wore a thoughtful look on her face.

"Don't give him ideas," I warned. "I told him we can't pay a ghost in cash either."

"I don't need cash," said Mart. "I can accept payment in the form of hot showers or old episodes of *Doctor Who*."

"I like both those things, so if that's an option…" Jia trailed off when Allie approached the bar. "Hey, Allie."

Jia liked *Doctor Who*, did she? I'd have to seriously refrain from getting my hopes up after previous experience, but I was starting to see why Allie had been so convinced she'd be a good fit.

"You're settling in okay?" She looked between us, a knowing glint in her eye. "Can I have a word with Maura for a second?"

"Sure." I stepped out from behind the bar and followed her until I was sure Jia was out of earshot. "Did you know she can see ghosts?"

"That's one reason I thought you two would get on."

The idea that she'd taken me into consideration when picking my new co-worker warmed my cold heart, I had to admit. "I can see why you were confident in her."

Someone who could see my brother *and* had experience in bartending was the ideal candidate. Not to mention her previous conflict with Mina Devlin, which would mean she wouldn't turn on us if we ticked off the coven even further. Finally, a stroke of luck.

"Not every local witch was Mina's ally," she replied. "I'm glad she said yes, at any rate."

The rest of the morning passed without any issues. The restaurant wouldn't get too busy until lunchtime, but since Allie also had to work at the front desk and help her other guests at the inn, it was easier with two of us working at the bar instead of one.

It wasn't until close to lunchtime that my phone buzzed with a message from Drew. I removed my phone from my pocket and read his text: *Sorry, I had a late night. Can I drop by in a bit with an update?*

Sure, I replied.

If he came here, I might have to introduce him to Jia, but her trial shift ended at lunchtime. I had to admit I wished she'd stay for longer, but Allie re-entered the restaurant shortly before the lunchtime shift started. "Jia, your trial's over."

"That was fast," she commented. "Does this mean I got the job, then?"

"Absolutely," said Allie. "You're hired. Come with me, and I'll give you all the necessary paperwork to take back with you."

"See you soon." I waved her off and returned to the bar, resigning myself to talking to Drew while wrangling customers on the lunch shift.

Mart sighed behind me. "I'd just got used to someone aside from you being able to talk to me."

"She'll be back," I told him. "Soon you'll have someone to annoy who isn't me."

While I'd finished dealing with the first batch of

lunchtime customers, Drew entered the restaurant. He looked pretty tired, no doubt from spending half the night dealing with cranky werewolves. I wished there was something I could have done to help, but really, the best thing I could have done was getting as far away as possible.

"Hey." He sat down in front of the bar. "Sorry I missed your text. I more or less passed out as soon as I got home."

"Is everything okay?" I asked. "With the pack, I mean?"

He ran a hand over his forehead. "You probably heard yesterday that the victim was the would-be husband of the pack chief's youngest daughter. The death was classified as a murder, but it's likely to require a witch's or wizard's expertise to determine the cause of death. Unfortunately, the family won't release the body."

"Why not? Don't they want to know how he died?"

"They won't let a non-werewolf near him," he explained. "We typically bury our dead right away, so surrendering the body to be examined by a witch or wizard goes against our usual procedures. It doesn't help that the coven has mostly stayed out of shifter business."

"I bet." Tricky. "Mina Devlin isn't in control of the coven any longer, though."

"No, but deaths in the pack are typically straightforward to figure out," he said. "Murder, even more so. Usually, it's clear when a shifter kills another. This time, the cause might be magical."

I grimaced. "They don't think a non-shifter was responsible, do they? What do you think?"

"I think he was poisoned, personally," he answered. "But without getting any experts near the body, all we can do is guess."

"There must be another way."

"There is. Summoning his ghost."

I should have known. "You want me to do it?"

"Without witnesses," he clarified. "I've closed off the park—well, the area where the body was found, anyway. I know it's not ideal, but if his ghost can shed some light on who killed him, then we might not need to pressure the family to let the body be examined right away."

"The ghost can only be summoned soon after his death." Within a day. He might have already appeared, actually, but none of the shifters would be able to see him. "When do you need me to come?"

"As soon as you can. Are you still trialling your new bartender?"

"She went home, but I can come and help you after Carey gets back from school in a couple of hours. That okay?"

"Sure."

It wasn't ideal, but since werewolves couldn't see ghosts, it was up to me to deal with this one.

3

When I explained the situation to Allie, she was happy to let me go for a brief ghost-hunting venture with Drew after Carey got back from school.

"Nobody wants pack drama on their hands," she remarked. "I'll take over the restaurant while you're gone, since it's pretty quiet around that time of day. Carey won't mind keeping an eye on reception."

"Thanks," I said gratefully. "It's not ideal, but soon we'll have Jia to help us out."

"She'll be moving to town permanently in the next few days, I expect. If she has trouble finding a place, then I can always give her a room at the inn, if you don't mind."

"Are you kidding me? It's perfect."

I wasn't the type to immediately declare someone my new best friend, but I might have to make an exception for Jia. I certainly wished she'd been able to pick up some of the slack as I dealt with the lunchtime rush that day. Mart tried to help, but he was more of a hindrance than anything. I'd sent him into the kitchen to get him out from under my feet and then had to deal with complaints from the chefs about the ovens randomly turning themselves on and off.

"You're a menace, you are," I told him when he returned to the bar.

"I wanted to help out," he protested. "It's not my fault electrical appliances go all weird when I'm near them."

"A likely story. You did that on purpose to get my attention." I cast my mind around for ideas as to how to entertain him while still making him feel useful. "Tell you what, if you like the ovens so much, you can stay in the kitchen and give me signals whenever the chef has a meal ready for me to take to someone. Deal?"

"Deal."

Mart's signals mostly consisted of him doing ridiculous dances, but at least it gave him something to do which didn't involve turning off the appliances, accidentally dropping plates, or flooding the kitchen. I was feeling pretty good about our arrangement by the time Carey came back from school.

Allie walked over to relieve me of bar duty. "You're ready to head out?"

"Sure." I ducked out from behind the bar, removing my apron. "Hey, Carey."

"Hey," she said. "You're going out?"

"The detective needs my help with something related to the pack. I won't be more than an hour."

"Why does he need your help?" she asked. "Wait, does it involve a ghost?"

"It might." I definitely didn't want to take Carey anywhere near the pack if I could help it. "I don't think the detective wants me to tell you the details, but I'll ask if I can share anything later."

"Oh, sure." She reached down to stroke Casper when he sprang over, meowing at her. "Will you let me know if there's a chance to get some good ghost footage?"

"I will, but I have my doubts." I'd never had to deal directly with a werewolf ghost before, and I had trouble picturing one being cooperative enough to put on an entertaining show for the cameras. I'd be better off trying to solve the murder first, anyway.

I hurried up to my room to change out of my work clothes—I'd make the most of the brief time I got to spend with Drew, even if we'd likely have a ghost as a third wheel—before heading back downstairs.

After saying goodbye to Allie and Carey, I left the inn and walked across the bridge which led to the main part of town. The river surged below the bridge, the waters high, but thankfully no ghosts ambushed me on my way across.

The spirit I'd helped yesterday had moved on happily enough once I'd fulfilled his request, but sometimes I felt distinctly like a protagonist in a video game forced to do mundane and annoying tasks in order to progress to the next level. Except all my progression had stopped when I'd quit the Reapers, so I was stuck in an endless loop. Not that I regretted my choice, but I had to admit part of me was glad Drew had trusted me to help solve this case.

Murders weren't more common in Hawkwood Hollow than other towns of a similar size, but theoretically, the event which had caused the river to overflow might count as a mass murder if it was ever proven that it hadn't been an accident. Since only Harold the Reaper shared my suspicions and he'd immediately ordered me never to tell another soul, I hadn't even told Drew or Allie.

Jia might have some idea, but I hadn't wanted to start off her first trial shift by dropping that bombshell on her. Her own grudge against Mina Devlin didn't mean she'd immediately believe my claims about an event I hadn't even been present for, and besides, I didn't have time to lead a crusade against the former coven leader who might have vanished off the face of the earth, for all we knew. I had more than enough problems of my own—like the werewolves.

In daylight, it was slightly easier for me to track down the right place to meet Drew outside the park entrance, and thankfully, there were no signs of any stargazing wannabe Seers in the bushes this time around.

"Hey." Drew strode over to meet me. "Glad you could make it over. This shouldn't take long, since I know you're needed at work."

"Allie was happy to take over from me for a bit, and I can't complain about getting outside," I replied. "Wait, does the victim's family know I'm going to contact his ghost?"

"Not exactly," he answered. "They're the ones who are refusing to release his body to the police. It's their fellow pack members who are stirring up trouble and passing rumours around, so talking to his ghost ought to put a stop to that, at the very least."

I hoped he was right. "Where do you want me to do this, then? In the park?"

"Yes, we can find an isolated area of the park in which to summon his ghost, if that works for you."

In truth, it didn't necessarily matter where I did the summoning, but I'd come all this way, and the park had plenty of cover to avoid nosy onlookers.

"I shouldn't need any props to do the summoning," I explained. "Not if I have permission to use my Reaper powers, anyway."

"From me?" Drew raised a brow. "Absolutely. Nobody is going to report you."

I didn't normally make a habit of using my Reaper powers to contact ghosts—usually they came to me instead—but in some cases, one needed to be persuasive. And if the victim's family wouldn't let the detective into their home, they definitely wouldn't let me snoop around searching for their son's ghost. I'd be better off keeping my distance and using the most direct method, so I followed Drew deeper into the park.

As we walked, I kept one eye open for any interlopers, but aside from a few shifter kids playing on swings and seesaws, I didn't see anyone who raised my suspicions. "We need to make sure nobody wanders past and gets freaked out when they see my shadows."

Given that Drew himself had seen my Reaper skills up close more than once, it still surprised me that he hadn't run for the hills. Even among paranormals, the ability to summon up creepy shadows was hardly standard, and Reapers rarely let others in on their secrets.

Yet Drew had accepted mine.

"I'll keep an eye out, don't worry," he reassured me. "Will there be any other potential issues?"

"I can't promise I'll be able to get any definite answers," I told him in an undertone. "Ghosts aren't reliable witnesses, even to their own deaths, most of the time. But I'll do my best."

If the victim had died by poisoning, he might not remember the circumstances, which meant it'd be harder to pin down the culprit than if he'd been attacked by another werewolf. On the other hand, in the latter case, he'd have likely seen his attacker anyway, rendering the need for a Reaper unnecessary.

Drew rounded a corner and muttered a curse under his breath. "We have company."

A woman with curly blond hair stepped out in front of us. Her eyes were red rimmed, her arms folded across her broad chest. "So this is the Reaper?"

Uh-oh. Had Drew told them about me? Judging by his evident surprise, I'd guess not. "Who are you?"

"Maura, this is Shana Quinn," said Drew. "The fiancée of the victim."

"Yes, Davey and I were due to be married this weekend." She spoke in accusing tones. "When you mentioned that you were going to consult with someone, I knew exactly who you meant. She was here at the park yesterday, wasn't she? The Reaper Witch."

I studied her, apprehension prickling up my spine. "Yes, I was, for a brief time. I'm sorry for your loss."

"No, you aren't," she said bluntly. "You witches don't care about the pack, and I doubt Reapers do either. Anyway, Detective, you didn't even consult with me beforehand."

"I tried to." Drew spoke in calm tones. "Your father refused to listen. I realise that he's the pack chief, but I'm the leading detective, and it's my job to find answers for you. There's a limited amount of time after someone's death in which their ghost might be contacted, so I brought Maura here in the hopes of getting you some answers."

She glowered at me. "Well, I don't appreciate it. We don't need witches *or* Reapers shoving their noses into our business."

It seemed that I'd have to persuade her myself. While her anger was understandable, if she insisted on being an obstructionist for the sake of it, I'd have to choose whether it was worth ticking her off rather than risking open conflict within the pack by neglecting to contact her fiancé's ghost.

"I'm not working for anyone," I informed her. "Not for a coven or for the Reapers. I'm doing this as a favour for Drew, nothing more."

"Really." Her narrowed eyes looked me over. "Not for your own gain?"

"I mean, it'll be an upside for all of us if the pack doesn't tear one another to pieces, but if you want the honest answer, then I want to finish my date with Drew that your pack drama interrupted. Does that sound like a fair deal?"

A faint flush spread across her cheekbones. "Fine, then. Get it over with."

I'd won the argument. Drew gave me a sideways look, half relieved and half exasperated, then led me the rest of the way to a clearing surrounded by bushes. I checked for any passers-by, but unless someone was lying in the undergrowth like a certain would-be Seer, nobody was watching us.

"How does this work?" Shana asked. "Will the rest of us be able to see his ghost as well?"

"I'll use my Reaper skills to look into the afterworld and see if his ghost is around," I explained. "As for whether you can see him or not, it depends if you're brave enough to get up close and personal with the dead."

She gave me a sceptical look. "Really? That sounds too wishy-washy for my taste."

There was nothing remotely wishy-washy about the afterworld, but she'd see that for herself soon enough. "Don't you want to know the truth about how Davey died?"

"He was murdered. I don't need to speak to his ghost to know that."

"Then you can hear the truth directly from him." If he wanted to speak to her, that is, which depended on whether she'd been involved in his murder or not. I hoped Drew had considered that possibility.

She worked her jaw. "Only if you let me talk to him alone."

Oh, great. Now she was adding conditions. Why had I agreed to do this again? I didn't summon ghosts on command. Yes, I'd started to get bolder about using my Reaper abilities after I'd found out definitively that the Reaper Council intended to leave me alone for the time being, but that didn't mean I wasn't asking for trouble by offering to summon a ghost as part of a police investigation.

"That's not part of the deal," I told her. "You're welcome to stick around, but my priority is finding the murderer. The word of the victim is enough proof for the police, right?"

Drew inclined his head. "If you want justice, let Maura work."

She didn't look convinced, but she didn't voice any more protests. I stepped into the middle of the small clearing, putting as much distance between myself and the others as possible, before summoning the shadows.

Shana sucked in a breath, and her alarmed expression disappeared beneath a mask of shadows that swept from underneath my feet.

I peered into the darkness in search of any bright spots which indicated the presence of a ghost.

"Hello?" I called out. "Davey Rogers?"

No response came. It hit me with a chill that my Reaper senses hadn't reacted when he'd died the previous night. Weird. I'd thought that using my powers on a frequent basis had made them more reactive, but if I'd sensed Davey's death while I'd been wandering around the park looking for Drew, I would have noticed.

"Davey?" I called his name again, but the darkness remained absolute. He wasn't here.

The shadows folded outward, revealing Shana's startled face. "Where is he?"

"I can't find him. If I had to guess, he's already moved on."

"Moved on?" she echoed.

"To the afterlife. The next world. Whichever." I might have put it in a more delicate way, but she'd hardly helped my efforts to find her fiancé's ghost. I was more annoyed at the spirit himself, but her disdain grated on me, to say the least.

Shana's eyes narrowed. "So this was a waste of time?"

"Not necessarily," I replied. "At least we know he's not here. Witches are more used to the possibility of becoming a ghost after death, but shifters don't always stick around."

"Is there another way to summon his ghost?" asked Drew. "Using a spell?"

"I can try that, but I'd need to drop by the apothecary first to pick up some props."

Shana sniffed. "I thought witches carried their props with them at all times."

Some did, but I wasn't exactly an ordinary witch, and I wasn't a normal Reaper either. Maybe I'd hoped for too much when I'd expected my summoning to work, but I didn't want to meet Drew's eyes in case I saw disappointment looking back at me.

"I didn't come here expecting to do that kind of summoning," I told Shana. "Besides, if I couldn't locate him using my Reaper senses, he's far more likely to have moved on."

She studied me, her jaw tensed. Despite her stoic expression, she had to be hurting pretty badly. "Then there's no point, is there?"

"There are other ways to get answers," Drew said. "Starting with questioning everyone who saw Davey before his death."

Including Shana herself. She was the pack chief's daughter, too, which I'd admittedly forgotten.

Shana grunted. "Does she have to come?"

"Maura will accompany me, yes." *In case his ghost shows up.* I filled in the blanks. If Shana guessed, though, she didn't say.

"I'll take you to see my dad, then." She left the clearing, and Drew and I followed her. "He's not in the best of moods, so it's anyone's guess how he'll take it when you tell him you tried to summon Davey's ghost."

"The marriage was a pack arrangement, right?" I asked. "Was it his idea?"

"Yes, mutually agreed upon by our families," she said. "I did care for him, though. Enough that I hope they catch the murderer who did it. To tell you the truth, I'd like to get my teeth in them myself."

Okay... "Do you have any ideas about who might have had a reason to kill him?"

"Meaning me?" She scowled. "The detective already asked. No, I didn't kill my would-be husband. Do you have any idea how expensive this wedding has been?"

"No, I'm asking you questions to know what I'm getting myself into." Kind of true. I'd never met the pack chief before, but even Drew would have to surrender authority to Shana's father, which wouldn't play in my favour if he turned out to object to my ghost-hunting ways.

I did want to rule her out as a potential suspect, but I also wanted to know if the rest of her family was likely to stand in my way—and the detective's too. If Drew had already questioned her, he must have struck her from his personal suspect list. I didn't know if she'd truly loved her soon-to-have-been husband, and I remembered Drew saying she'd got cold feet the previous day, but there were ways to call off a wedding that didn't involve murder.

She struck me as honest to the point of being blunt, but I wasn't good at reading people in general, and shifters were pretty different than witches and wizards and other paranormals I'd dealt with. Then again, from my experience with Drew, werewolves were also more open and straightforward than the gossipy coven members.

Shana, Drew and I reached the other side of the park and made our way down a cul-de-sac of pleasant-looking, terraced houses. Shana took the lead, bringing us to an impressive manor house behind a large fence. "Here we are."

It was time for me to meet the chief of the werewolves.

4

The chief of the werewolves certainly lived in luxury. His house was bigger than the entire Riverside Inn, with fences circling expansive grounds, and while I didn't see any security cameras, he probably didn't need any with several werewolves living on the property.

Shana pulled out a key before unlocking the front door.

"You're back already?" a female voice called from the other side.

"Yes, and the detective is here," Shana answered.

"Is he now?" The sound of a door shutting came from somewhere inside the house. "You should have warned us. Your father is outside. I'll fetch him."

Her footsteps faded into the distance, while the detective and I hovered awkwardly on the doorstep.

"You live with your parents, then?" I asked Shana to fill the silence. "With the pack chief? Is that typical?"

Shana gave me a blistering look. "My fiancé and I were

going to move into our own house after the wedding, but now that's not going to happen. I'm a full-time student, so I can't afford to rent a place of my own yet."

"Just curious." I'd be reluctant to move out of a fancy house like this one, and it struck me that she was pretty young to be getting married. She couldn't be older than twenty-one or so.

Footsteps echoed from inside the house, and a woman with dark-blond hair walked into view. She had the same tall, strong build as Shana did, but her features were softer, without the stubborn set to the jaw that her daughter had. "He's ready to see you now."

Apprehension built inside me as Drew and I walked through a large foyer and into a wide sitting room furnished in polished wood. A powerfully built man with greying blond hair sat in an armchair as if it was a throne, and his blue eyes held the hint of a challenge as they swept over Drew and me. "I wasn't aware you were bringing company, Detective."

"Chief Quinn, this is Maura." He gestured towards me. "Maura, this is Chief Quinn."

The chief indicated for us to sit down on one of the plush sofas. "I would have appreciated being informed of your visit in advance."

I sank into the plush cushion, which forced me to look up at the chief even more than I already had to.

"I did mention I would drop by later this afternoon." Drew didn't sit down. "Maura and I encountered your daughter in the park, and she gave us the impression that you were open to visitors. Are you expecting anyone else?"

"Not currently." The chief beckoned, and his wife and

daughter entered the room. "Let us begin, then. Why did you bring a witch in here?"

"She's not just a witch, Dad." Shana didn't sit next to her mother, instead meeting her father's eyes. "She's a Reaper."

So much for getting off on the right foot. I straightened my spine so that I felt less like I was sinking into the sofa while the chief looked down at me.

"A Reaper," he repeated. "I wasn't aware the town had a new one."

"I'm not an official Reaper." I perched on the edge of the seat. Not the most comfortable pose but better than practically lying on my back.

Drew spoke. "Maura came here to offer her assistance in solving the matter of Davey's untimely death."

Shana's hands clenched at her sides, but she otherwise showed no emotion. Neither of her parents looked particularly grief-stricken, either, but it sounded like the marriage had been based in pack politics more than genuine attachment.

"She tried to summon his ghost," Shana told her parents. "It didn't work."

"You tried to *what?*" Mrs Quinn's jaw dropped, and even her husband arched a brow in surprise. *Thanks for that one, Shana.*

"I can see and talk to ghosts," I explained. "I'm told his death is causing a lot of strife in the pack, so Drew and I decided the quickest way to solve the matter was to talk to the man himself."

The chief's blue eyes studied me. "Was that your decision to make?"

Well... no. The way Shana had delivered the news

before we'd had the chance to work up to the subject wasn't ideal, because it automatically made Drew and me sound like busybodies who'd acted behind the chief's back.

"Your daughter gave us permission," I told him. "I explained that the most likely time to find a ghost is within twenty-four hours of his death, so she allowed me to give it a try. When his ghost didn't appear, the detective and I came here instead."

While part of me had briefly wondered if Davey Rogers's ghost was roaming around their property instead, I had my doubts that he'd be haunting the pack chief's home if he hadn't lived here. I could certainly use my Reaper skills to see if there were any ghosts in the building, but not in front of an audience.

"You gave her permission, did you?" The chief looked at his daughter, who stared defiantly back. "But she was unsuccessful."

I fidgeted, annoyance rising at the ghost's elusiveness. "It's not an exact art. It just means the detective will have to find the culprit the old-fashioned way."

"Precisely," said Drew. "I thought I'd start here because you were the one who suggested the match, were you not, Chief?"

Mrs Quinn lifted her chin. "Actually, it was me."

Her husband's jaw twitched. "You made the suggestion to me first, then we told Shana."

"What were your reasons for opting for a pack marriage, exactly?" Drew asked. "Shana is your youngest daughter, correct?"

"And my heir," added the chief. "If she is to take my place one day, she will need to have strong connections with other pack families, which can be achieved by making the right match."

"And did you know from the start that Davey Rogers would be amenable to marrying your daughter?" Drew enquired.

"We thought he'd require some persuasion," said Mrs Quinn.

Shana scoffed. "Yeah, right. His parents were less than thrilled from the get-go."

Interesting. What would put them off being linked to the pack chief's family? I didn't know nearly enough about shifter politics to guess what possible advantages that position might give them, but I'd rather not expose my ignorance in front of people who didn't seem to like me much anyway.

Chief Quinn gave his daughter a warning look. "Davey Rogers's parents weren't keen to push their son into a pack marriage at first, but they came around to the idea when he said yes."

"Hardly." Shana scoffed. "They kept trying to convince him otherwise even after we set the wedding date. His brother too."

"You and Davey already knew one another?" Drew asked. "Before the arrangement?"

"Of course we did," she said. "Everyone in the pack knows everyone else. *You* know that, but I suppose you're asking for your companion's benefit."

What was her problem with me? Or was she just trying to rile up her parents? The combination of their disdain and her snide comments made me want to leave them to their bickering, but it baffled me that they'd decided on their daughter's future without her input.

Especially as the pack chief was supposed to be voted in by the rest of the pack, not given his title through the family line like the monarchy.

"I'm the chief investigator on the case, which means I might have to ask obvious questions to gain a bigger picture of the events which led to Davey's death." Drew's tone was measured, but a muscle ticked in his jaw, as if their disdain towards me was annoying him too. "You and Davey were childhood friends. Were you close before the arrangement?"

"No," answered Mrs Quinn. "They hadn't spoken in years."

Shana glared at her mother. "It wasn't like we never saw one another. We've lived in the same part of town for our whole lives."

"So you sent the request to Davey's parents, correct?" Drew asked. "You invited them to speak with you?"

The chief inclined his head. "We often met to discuss various pack matters, and at one such meeting, the subject of our children came up. They are—were—the same age, so it was only natural that we'd want what was best for them."

Shana made a sceptical noise, only to be silenced by another warning look from her mother. She didn't seem thrilled at the notion of her parents dictating her future—understandable enough, but why had she agreed to the arrangement to begin with?

"What did Davey's parents say, then?" asked Drew.

"His father said that he'd ask Davey, but he was reluctant to make a commitment," the chief continued. "It's my understanding that they wanted their son to have the freedom to choose his partner for himself."

"How... modern." Mrs Quinn wrinkled her nose. Was that supposed to be a bad thing? Apparently so. Maybe she'd been shoved into marriage with the chief in the same manner.

"But they came around, Davey agreed, and then?" Drew pressed. "How long passed between your initial request and the wedding itself?"

"Does it matter?" asked Shana.

"Six months," said Chief Quinn.

That seemed fast, but then again, shifters had different views on how long courtship was meant to last than witches did, especially when it came to marriages designed to strengthen pack relations.

"Did Davey express any doubts in recent weeks?" asked Drew.

"None aside from the usual," Mrs Quinn replied.

Drew, however, had his eyes on her daughter. "Did you witness him show any second thoughts, Shana? You spent more time with him than anyone else did, I'm sure."

"Doubts?" She gave a brittle laugh. "He doubted everything. He dithered over the wedding date for weeks, and frankly, I was convinced he'd run off as soon as we got to the altar."

Hmm. "Did you know he'd gone out yesterday evening?"

"No." She lowered her gaze. "I was at home. I didn't... didn't know."

Her oddly vulnerable demeanour contrasted her former attitude, but nothing pointed to obvious guilt either.

"Were you two at home too?" I asked her parents.

"Yes," said the chief. "My wife was with me. Shana was upstairs in her room."

No doubt they wouldn't appreciate me asking probing questions, but I had my doubts that any of them had been involved in Davey's death, regardless. They wouldn't jeopardise their own pack status when they were the ones who'd suggested the marriage to begin with, would they? Besides, I hadn't seen any of them at the park when Davey's body had been unearthed.

In any case, I had an inkling that we weren't going to get a confession from either of them. Apparently thinking along similar lines, Drew abandoned that line of questioning. "Shana is a full-time student, right?"

"Yes, she's studying at that local academy." Mrs Quinn answered in rather haughty tones. "The one run by witches."

An interesting choice for a werewolf, but as far as I knew, the town had only one higher-education institute.

"Do you know what you want to do afterwards?" I addressed Shana.

She glowered at me. "Is that relevant?"

Maybe not, but she clearly wasn't happy living at home, and her parents' disapproval of her choices stood out starkly. I understood wanting to get away, since I'd had the same desire myself until Mart's death and the implosion of my Reaper training had made the decision for me. I wouldn't have gone as far as to marry someone I didn't care for, though.

"I need to have all the details," Drew told her. "Who else was invited to the wedding? Anyone who might have objected to your union?"

"Everyone was invited," said the chief. "If you plan to

question every single shifter in town, then it'll take a while."

Drew gave him an assessing look. "Did anyone decline the invitation?"

A moment of tension passed among all three of them. Then Shana spoke up. "My sister and I had a disagreement, so I took her off the guest list. She didn't mind."

She had a sister? That was something that would have been useful to know earlier on. "Is she younger than you?"

The chief rose to his feet. "My eldest child has chosen to distance herself from the pack altogether, which makes Shana my heir."

And her sister refused to come to the wedding?

"A disagreement?" Drew asked. "Was this about the wedding itself?"

"That's irrelevant." Mrs Quinn gave a nervous glance at her husband. "Tessa is… she's prone to trying to stir up trouble."

Reading between the lines, I wouldn't get far by questioning Shana any further about her older sibling while her parents were in the room. Drew seemed to think so, too, because he motioned towards the door. "I see. If you don't have any more information to give me, then I will take my leave."

"Do that," growled the chief. "When we catch the killer, they will regret crossing my family."

I wasn't sorry to leave the room with Drew, while Shana seized the chance to slip away too.

I waylaid her when her parents were out of earshot. "About your sister…"

"Drop it," she said in a low voice. "Unless you want to put my dad in a raging temper, that is."

"I want to know who killed your would-be husband, that's all. Why did you argue with your sister?"

"We argued because she thought I was wasting my time getting married at all and it wouldn't achieve anything." She gave a bitter laugh. "You think she killed Davey? I doubt it. She uses words rather than actions to undermine our family."

"Thanks for answering our questions." Drew pushed open the front door and stepped outside.

"Glad I could help." Her tone brimmed with maximum insincerity. "Do tell us if you plan to contact his ghost again, won't you?"

"I doubt that'll be an option." Unfortunately.

As we left the house, I reached out with my Reaper senses, but I didn't sense any ghosts in the vicinity. As I'd thought, Davey wasn't haunting the pack chief or his family.

Drew gave me a quizzical look. "Were you looking for ghosts?"

"You caught me." I flashed him a quick smile. "Ghosts usually take refuge in places familiar to them or where they feel comfortable, though. Frankly, I doubt anyone feels comfortable in there."

He glanced over his shoulder at the house. "Tread carefully around the chief. He's temperamental, but he wields a strong influence over the pack."

"His daughter didn't seem inclined to tread carefully around him," I pointed out. "And what about her mysterious older sister? Did you know about her?"

"Yes, but I didn't know they were in contact," he said. "To my knowledge, she lives outside of the town."

"So you don't have her address." If she was a potential

suspect, then it might be worth pursuing that line of questioning. "I guess the chief wouldn't be happy if we paid her a visit?"

"No, but it's not a bad idea. I'll have to head to the police station first and see if I can find her contact details."

Drew and I retraced our steps out of shifter territory towards the main high street. While the police station was located in the witches' area of town, most of the local police force were shifters of some kind or other, with only a few witches and wizards on the team. The redbrick building stood apart from its neighbours, and when Drew approached the automatic doors, I halted on the threshold.

"You want to go back to the inn?" he guessed.

I checked the time. I'd been gone for far longer than I'd planned, but if the chief's wayward daughter turned out to be a threat, I didn't want him to go after her alone.

"Tell you what, I'll drop by the apothecary while you get Tessa's address and get some herbs for a ghost summoning. I can ask if anyone has bought any poisons or something similar too."

"If the killer is a werewolf, I doubt they bought poison from an apothecary."

I blinked. "You think they brewed it themselves?"

"It's more likely that they used wild plants or herbs instead."

That made sense. "It's worth buying some herbs anyway, to see if I can snag that elusive ghost."

"Sure, go ahead. I'll get Shana's sister's contact details and see if she's willing to talk."

"I'll let you know how it goes."

I turned away from the police station and made for the local apothecary. It was actually my first time going there since the former owner had been murdered and Mina Devlin had tried to cover up the crime. The windows were boarded up and the door locked. I'd have thought the coven would have found a replacement by now, but the new healer was an employee at the local hospital, and the rest of the coven wasn't exactly at its best after the departure of its former leader.

I peered through the grimy windows. The apothecary didn't look like it'd even been restocked since its abandonment, so it'd be a waste of time using my Reaper skills to sneak in and grab the ingredients I needed. Giving up, I returned to the police station to wait for Drew.

Several minutes later, the automatic doors slid open, and he reappeared.

"I got the address," he told me. "Tessa Quinn lives on a farm north of Hawkwood Hollow, but she isn't answering the phone. Did you get your ingredients?"

"No, the apothecary is closed," I said. "I guess they didn't find anyone to replace poor old Angie."

"There must be other places for you to get those herbs for a summoning, surely."

"I imagine the coven has its own stores, but do you think they'd let me borrow them after what I did?" They'd either laugh in my face or hex me. Or both.

"Can't you use your Reaper skills to sneak in?"

"If I get caught, then Mina's cronies will eat me alive." I could ask Jia if she knew any alternatives, but since she'd left for home, that'd have to wait until later.

In the meantime, Drew and I made our way north. I hadn't realised the shifters' territory stretched so far, but the entire northwest section of town belonged to them, and so did a fair few of the fields and farms which bordered the upper edges of Hawkwood Hollow. A long country road continued past the town's boundary, which we followed until we neared an isolated farm nestled between two fields.

When we turned off the path and approached the house, a loud growl sounded, as if in warning. Then a werewolf bore down on us, teeth bared, ready to attack.

5

"**S**top," Drew commanded.

The werewolf stopped midcharge, growling loudly at Drew. I hoped it was because she recognised his authority, because I'd hardly come prepared for a battle with an enraged werewolf. I reached into my pocket for my wand while Drew and the werewolf had an intense stare-off for a few long seconds. Thankfully, before anyone could come to blows, the wolf shifted into a blond woman—unclothed, of course. I politely averted my gaze while she grabbed a long robe to cover herself with before straightening upright. Her blond hair and broad frame made her immediately recognisable as Shana's sister and the chief's daughter.

"Detective," Tessa said in a raspy voice. "I thought you were a trespasser. Who's she?"

"I'm Maura," I said. "I'm helping Drew with his ongoing investigation into Davey Rogers's murder."

Her shoulders tensed under her robe, but at least she didn't shift into a wolf again. "Murder, you say?"

"I'm sure you've heard by now that your sister's fiancé died yesterday evening," Drew said. "I'm the detective in charge of the case."

"I'm aware of that." She looked us over, her gaze lingering on me for a moment. "I might live out in the middle of nowhere, but I've hardly been living under a rock. What do you want with me?"

"We're here to ask you a few questions," Drew told her. "It shouldn't take long if you cooperate. I tried to call you earlier, but you didn't answer the phone."

"Oh, I don't answer any unknown number."

"If you did, it might tip you off about visitors." I probably shouldn't try to provoke her, but her ambush had set my nerves on edge, especially given her sister's claim that she preferred using her words rather than actions.

"Fine," she growled. "Come in."

Someone wasn't accustomed to giving visitors a warm welcome, that was for sure. The ramshackle farmhouse behind her was a far cry from the chief's fancy abode, but much cosier, with rugs covering the wooden floor, a fire burning in the grate, and a considerable amount of hair on the furniture. Did she spend most of her time in wolf form? Possibly she did. I could understand why she'd picked this life over a pack marriage with someone she didn't love, but did her disdain for pack politics extend to sabotaging her sister's wedding by murdering the groom?

Tessa sat down on the rug, her robe displaying rather more skin than necessary. To my relief, Drew kept his eyes on her face. "Thank you for agreeing to speak to us. Your sister mentioned that you declined an invitation to her wedding."

Tessa made a disparaging noise. "I suppose she

thought it amusing to tell you I was the one who killed her fiancé."

"Actually, she was pretty adamant that you didn't," I ventured. "She also told us that you claimed the marriage wouldn't last and that it was doomed to failure."

"Then why would you peg me as a suspect?" she asked.

"I thought it necessary to get your perspective on the matter," said Drew. "Were you always opposed to their relationship?"

"They didn't have a relationship." She gave an eye roll. "It was entirely put together by our parents, and she went along because she's incapable of making her own decisions."

That wasn't the impression I'd got, but I supposed she knew Shana better than I did.

"Did you meet Davey yourself?" asked Drew.

"I know him, same as the rest of the pack, but we haven't really spoken in the past year."

That made it unlikely she'd talked to him without her sister's knowledge, especially given her remote location. If she was telling the truth, that is.

"Do you know of anyone else who might have wanted to call off the wedding?" I asked.

"Everyone on Davey's side of the pack, for a start, since it was my parents' idea to placate an old rival and his supporters." She yawned. "Davey himself wasn't interesting enough to provoke anyone into murdering him, so I assume it was politically motivated."

"How many supporters does he have, exactly?" I tensed when she looked directly at me.

"I didn't count them. Why are you helping Drew? You're not a shifter."

Drew cleared his throat. "No, Maura is…"

"A Reaper," I finished. "I hoped to find Davey's ghost, but it didn't work out, so I'm helping with the questioning instead."

Her brows shot up. "A Reaper? I thought the last one retired."

"It's not my official title." I was also getting slightly fed up with justifying my presence at Drew's side. Did the shifters always react in this way when someone from the other side of town stepped into their territory? "Can we get back to the point? It's not exactly practical for Drew to question every single person who might have opposed their match, so we could use some more direction."

Her lips pursed. "I'm not the person to ask for specifics. I moved out here when I inherited the farmhouse from my grandparents on my mother's side, and I'm more than happy to stay out of their arguments."

Hmm. I didn't know if she was telling the truth, but out of everyone in the family, she lived the farthest from the place where Davey had died. I hadn't seen any ghosts out here at all, in fact. They preferred crowded places to remote locations most of the time.

"So you never wanted to succeed the chief?" I asked. "Or marry within the pack yourself?"

"Now you're just being nosy."

"We need to gain an understanding of how Davey and Shana found themselves in the position they were in," Drew said. "Besides, you can give us a useful outside perspective on the pack as a whole."

Not an unbiased one, though, but what did I expect from the pack chief's estranged daughter? "I frankly don't give a crap what you do," I told Tessa. "I have no skin in this game. I told your sister the same."

"Did you now." She gave me a considering look. "Then you got involved... why?"

"I'm dating the detective." If she hadn't already guessed, then there was no point in keeping it under wraps. While I detested using my romantic status to gain leverage, it was plain to see that nothing short of the approval of a shifter would command respect around here.

She looked more surprised than she had when I'd revealed I was a Reaper. "Are you? Does he normally bring his romantic partners to question murder suspects?"

"I was initially supposed to find Davey's ghost, which I already told you." I was also starting to wish I'd gone back to the inn instead. "Then I wondered if he was haunting someone in particular, but I don't have to be a genius to know he wouldn't set foot in here whether he was dead or alive."

She stared at me for a moment. Then she burst out laughing. "I bet the chief enjoyed meeting you."

Drew leaned forward. "To return to the matter at hand, a man is dead, his family is refusing to release the body for examination, and the pack stands on a knife's edge. Anything you might be able to give us might make a difference."

Tessa leapt to her feet, flashing yet more skin. Not in an obvious ploy for the detective's attention—she simply had a shifter's non-existent concept of modesty. "Look, if you ask me, it was one of his own people who did it to him."

I frowned. "Not his family, surely."

"He was an annoying fool, so it's no big loss," she said. "He hero-worshiped my sister, though. I think that's why she went along with it. She wants to be adored."

"Does she now?" Interesting. "Your parents don't seem to respect her very much."

"There's a reason I got out," she said. "She wouldn't listen to me when I told her to do the same. My opinion wasn't welcome."

"And what were you doing last night?" asked Drew. "Just for the record?"

"I was hunting in the woods." She gave a wolfish grin, and I decided I didn't want to know the details. "I don't know who killed him, but I'm glad Shana gets a second chance to make her own choice. I hope she doesn't squander it this time."

That seemed a little callous to me, but I'd got the distinct impression that she'd spent years clashing with the pack chief. I didn't blame her for not wanting to insert herself into pack drama again.

"Thanks for answering our questions." Drew led the way out of the room, while I turned my back on Tessa with relief.

"I don't think she's the killer," I remarked to Drew in an undertone as we left the farmhouse. "She doesn't strike me as subtle. Or patient."

"The chief's family members seem to have those traits in common," he agreed. "It was worth hearing her perspective, I think."

"Yeah, but blaming the victim's family seems a bit harsh," I commented. "Have you spoken to them today?"

"Not since yesterday," he said. "Unfortunately, they're still refusing to surrender the body for examination."

"Want me to help convince them?" On second thought, I'd ticked off enough shifters today already. "Joking, joking. Allie will think I'm skipping work if I don't get back to the inn soon."

"You should head back before it gets dark," he agreed. "With everyone on edge here, loitering near the park isn't a good idea."

"Knowing what they think of non-shifters now, I agree."

He grimaced. "This isn't typical behaviour. One of their own was murdered, and that results in pretty strong feelings."

"I think Tessa would have chased us off without needing an excuse. Anyway, I'll see you later."

"Sure, I'll message you." He gave me a brief kiss on the cheek as a goodbye. "I do want to resume our date. To be clear."

"Good." I flashed him a brief smile and departed. While I worried a little about leaving him alone in shifter territory, he'd be better off dealing with the bereaved family himself. This was far outside the scope of what I'd offered to help with, especially without a single ghost to be seen.

Upon reaching the high street, my gaze fell on the witches' headquarters. Like the apothecary, I hadn't set foot in the place since the departure of the former coven leader, and besides, I wasn't certain of the location where they kept their ingredient supplies.

The headquarters wasn't sealed to the public, but the bronze griffins on the exterior seemed to glare down at me as if they knew I didn't belong there. As I neared the doors, they sprang open, and none other than Belinda Jennings walked out—the stargazer who I'd run into the previous day.

"Oh, hello." She flashed me a vague smile. "It's you again."

"I didn't know you were in the coven."

"I'm not," she said brightly. "I sometimes offer advice to them, though. The input of a Seer is very valuable to some."

Uh-huh. I was sure Mina Devlin hadn't appreciated her input in the slightest, but if Belinda was allowed to wander into their headquarters, it must be open to nonmembers. Except, perhaps, the person who'd driven out their leader.

"I don't suppose you know if the apothecary is going to reopen anytime soon?"

She fixed a wide-eyed stare on me. "I'm afraid I cannot see that far ahead."

Or rather, she didn't know. "Okay. Never mind."

As I sidestepped her, she called out, "Did you know they found a dead body in the park?"

"Yes, I was there," I reminded her. "And so were you, remember? We ran into each other right before his body was found."

Come to think of it, had she seen anything at the scene of the crime? If she'd been hiding in the bushes all evening, then it was entirely possible she'd been present when the killer had disposed of the body, but whether she'd paid any attention was another matter entirely.

"You know what I think?" Her voice dropped to a

conspiratorial whisper. "Nobody else has said so, but I think his death was murder."

"Everyone thinks it was murder." And if anyone could witness a murder without noticing, it was her. "Also, if nobody's talking about it, how did you find out?"

She blinked at me. "I saw it coming, obviously. Stark as the moon."

"Right." I bloody well hoped she hadn't been telling tales to the witches. She wasn't exactly all there, but I didn't need her spreading unwanted rumours about the police's capacity to solve the case. Drew was doing his best, considering the lack of any evidence and my failure to find Davey's ghost.

I gave up on the notion of entering the witches' headquarters for the time being and left Belinda standing at the side of the road. When I glanced over my shoulder, her expression looked slightly put out, but she didn't follow me. Turning off the high street, I followed the route back to the inn.

When I entered the reception area, I glimpsed Carey levitating plates through the restaurant and felt a twinge of guilt for leaving her and her mother to handle all the work by themselves.

"Hey, Maura." Carey returned from dropping off the plates in the kitchen. "I wondered where you got to."

"I'll get back to work. Sorry I left you for so long."

"It's been pretty quiet this evening."

I grabbed my apron and returned to the bar. "I know you have homework to do, though."

Carey took up a seat at a nearby table with her laptop. "Nah, I finished my homework. I do want to update my blog, though."

"With what?"

"Not sure yet." She eyed me. "My mum told me a were-wolf was murdered, you know. You don't have to hide things from me."

"I didn't know if the detective wanted me to share the details with anyone, but I guess the whole town knows by now." Despite Shana's professions to the contrary. "Drew and I got delayed looking for the victim's would-be sister-in-law, who lived way out in the middle of nowhere."

"So you didn't summon his ghost?"

"He never showed up." For what reason, I could only guess. "So we had to do the questioning the long way instead. We talked to the pack chief and his family."

"You met the head of the pack?" Her eyes rounded. "I've never seen him. How was he?"

"Annoying."

"Speak for yourself." Mart floated through the door into the restaurant from the inn's reception area. "I can't believe you ran off on me. I'm so starved for attention that I'm actually having to talk to the other ghosts."

"Chill out," I told him. "Soon Jia will be back here, so you can chat to your heart's content."

"Yes, she will." Carey followed my gaze to the spot where my brother's ghost hovered. "She hasn't found a permanent place to move to yet, but she offered to pick up a shift tomorrow."

"Oh, that's good news."

"Yes, it'll be easier with someone else to help out." Allie walked over to join me at the bar. "Not that I'm blaming you for wanting to help the detective, Maura. I heard the shifter's death caused quite a stir over there."

"He was supposed to be marrying the pack chief's

daughter," I explained. "His ghost didn't stick around, which sometimes happens with shifters."

It couldn't be my Reaper skills that were the problem, because they'd been perfectly functional the last time I'd used them. Davey must have quickly vanished into the afterlife, maybe to avoid the chief and his family. I didn't blame him, but I hoped that Drew had better luck with the victim's family than he did with them.

All the same, I was rather less enthusiastic about helping Carey plan ghost tours for the inn and instead busied myself dealing with customers until the evening shift came to an end. Mart tailed me, not speaking until we were alone on the stairs leading to the upper floor. "You're still in a bad mood, aren't you?"

"An inconclusive murder investigation tends to lower my mood, yes."

"That's not all." He drifted upstairs alongside me. "Why didn't the ghost show his face? You did look for him, right?"

"Yes, I did." I kept my tone even, but a bit of annoyance slipped through. "Why wouldn't I?"

"I thought you and the detective might have gone off to do *other* activities." He waggled his eyebrows.

"He was doing his job," I reminded him. "We hoped to cut the questioning short by finding the guy's ghost, but no luck. Also, I might mention that I was supposed to be at work too."

He pulled a face. "If you ask me, you might be in a better mood if you'd taken some time off for a tumble in the bushes in shifter territory."

"We can't all be eternally teenaged ghosts without any responsibilities."

"I have responsibilities." He spoke in a petulant tone. "Like keeping you alive. Yet you ran off without me."

"If you wanted to ogle naked shifters, you should have just told me."

"I thought you and the detective didn't—"

"Not him," I interrupted. "Look, Davey's ghost not showing up wouldn't be a red flag, but I didn't sense his death either. Would you call that strange?"

"You went years without picking up on anyone's deaths," he reminded me. "Until a few weeks ago, anyway."

"I guess," I relented. "Talking to Davey's ghost would have cleared up a lot of issues, though, regardless."

"Like whether he was murdered."

"I'd be surprised if he wasn't. Do you think I should ask the Reaper?"

"Harold?" Mart snorted. "Absolutely not. He never does anything for other people unless it's to his own benefit, and usually not even then."

True. Most of the time he threw things at me or outright ignored me when I went to his house. I didn't need to add an argument with the Reaper to the day's failures, so I put that option in the *last resort* pile and moved on.

6

The following morning, I woke up in a more optimistic mood than I probably had the right to, considering yesterday had mostly been a failure. After all, in one crucial way, it'd been a success, and soon Jia was due to show up for her first real shift at the inn. For the first time in weeks, I wouldn't be run off my feet from morning until evening, and neither would Allie, while Carey would be able to relax after school rather than helping out in the restaurant. Admittedly, Allie didn't force her daughter to help out, but Carey was a fifteen-year-old kid who deserved to have her own life.

Such was my mood that I didn't even mind discussing ghost tours with Carey over breakfast.

"We need to find some ghosts if we want to make tours a regular feature," I remarked. "Which is next on the agenda now that we have a new bartender."

"Are you going to ask them yourself?" She dug a spoon into her cereal. "I'd help, but you know… I can't see them."

"We'll figure it out," I told her. "Mart can volunteer, since he's starved for attention at the moment."

"Hey!" My brother folded his arms across his transparent chest. "I have better things to do than run trials for ghosts."

"Like using up all my hot water?" I rolled my eyes. "You have twice as much time as I do because you don't need to sleep."

"I worked very hard yesterday," he announced. "I'd like to start working in the kitchen permanently."

"If you behave yourself, you can keep giving me signals when the meals are ready." If Carey was confused by our exchange, she didn't say a word. "Only if you promise not to turn off the ovens."

"I promise," he said solemnly. "I like being near the ovens. I can almost feel the heat."

Carey pushed her cereal bowl away. "Did he say yes?"

"We're working on it." I gave him a stern look. "Come on, you told me that you like meeting new people. Why not find us some volunteers in one of your nightly flights around town?"

"I suppose I can keep an eye out," he said grudgingly.

At least debating over the inn's future as a ghost-tour site took my mind off the werewolf pack drama and the fact that I hadn't heard from Drew yet. Maybe it'd been another late night. I wouldn't mind knowing if Davey Rogers's family had agreed to release the body after all, but that wasn't the part of the investigation I was involved in. As I had to keep telling myself, I dealt with ghosts, not shifters. Honestly, after yesterday, I was glad of it.

Not long after Carey departed for school, Jia walked into the restaurant. Today, she wore a black T-shirt imprinted with a white font. As she approached the bar, I squinted to read the words—*The Sarcasm is Strong with This One.*

"I like the shirt," I told her.

"Hey, Maura." She bounded behind the bar to join me. "Ready for another day's work?"

"You won't be that enthusiastic once you've met the lunchtime regulars," I warned. "Mrs Terrence is a terror, but it'll be more bearable with two of us here."

"Three of us!" Mart shouted from behind the kitchen door.

I turned my back on the closed door. "Some of us are more useful than others."

"I asked Allie to put me on shifts five days a week," Jia told me. "Sound good?"

"Definitely. When are you moving here again?"

"This weekend," she replied. "It's a short journey here via broomstick, but I'll make a point not to land in the fields to the north next time."

"Why?" I wondered if she'd been chased off by Tessa or one of the other werewolves. "Did you run into trouble?"

"If by *trouble*, you mean a local nutcase, then yes. That Belinda Jennings was standing knee-deep in mud, and she ambushed me when I landed."

"Her?" What in the world had she been doing all the way up the fields on shifter territory? It was weird enough that I'd run into her near the coven's headquarters, but she was at least a witch despite not being a coven member. "I ran into her at the werewolves' park the other day. She told me she was stargazing, but she was trying to look at the night sky through a pair of binoculars with the lenses covered."

"She's a few twigs short of a broomstick," Jia agreed. "She thinks she's a Seer, but her only gift for prophecies is the self-fulfilling ones."

I snorted. "That would explain why she claimed that she saw me coming in a vision when I'd been walking in circles around her for ages looking for the right entrance to the park."

"Why were you at the werewolves' park, anyway?"

I'd managed to avoid mentioning the werewolves yesterday, but given my connection with Drew, it was inevitable that she'd find out soon enough. "I had a date with Detective Drew Gardener."

I figured I might as well tell her before the rumour mill reached her first. Meaning, my brother. He'd shown admirable restraint in not mentioning Drew during the previous morning's trial, really.

"Never." Her brows shot up. "When did that happen? He's been a bachelor forever."

"We've been seeing one another for a few weeks." I didn't know if she'd heard about the recent murder, but since she wasn't currently living in Hawkwood Hollow, she might have missed the news.

Mart interrupted by flying into the restaurant from the kitchen. "Hey, it's my favourite co-worker."

"Excuse me?" I gave him a pointed look.

"You're family, so you don't count."

Oh, boy. While it was refreshing to have someone else to distract his attention, if I kept on the subject of Drew, Mart was liable to start making his own comments on our relationship. At least when nobody could hear him, he couldn't share my embarrassing stories with anyone but the other ghosts.

"I thought you were on kitchen duty. Or looking for ghosts who want to be part of a tour."

"Ghost tours?" Jia asked. "I remember Carey mentioning that."

As Mart launched into an explanation, my phone started buzzing in my pocket. Drew was calling me. "Hang on, I need to take this call."

Jia gave me a curious look but nodded, and I ducked out from behind the bar and answered the phone.

"Hey, Drew. Something up?"

"I don't want to drag you away from work, but we had a breakthrough in the investigation," he said. "The family agreed to release the body, so I wondered if you'd like to come and do some more ghost hunting later today."

"I can ask Allie. I'll let you know if I can drop by on my lunch break."

"Sure. I imagine they'll have confirmed the cause of death by then."

Sorted. Not that I wanted to leave Jia alone for too long on her first full day working here, but she'd have Allie to help her. For all I knew, confirming Davey Rogers's cause of death might drag his ghost out of hiding. If I could procure some ingredients for a summoning, that is.

Just before my lunch break, I turned to Jia. "Is it okay if I take my break now? I have to run out to do a couple of errands."

"Sure," she said. "Something going on? You seem a bit distracted."

"I'm helping Drew with an ongoing police investigation," I admitted. "He needed me to speak to the ghost of a werewolf who they believe was murdered the other day."

"A werewolf ghost?" She tilted her head. "Do they appear in wolf form or human?"

"Human, usually." Of all the questions she might ask, that was not remotely near the top of my list. "Is that okay, then?"

"Sure, I can cover for you." A smile played on her mouth. "If it's a murder investigation you're needed for, I'm pretty sure it should take priority."

"Don't give her ideas," Mart warned. "She's always running off to investigate murders when she's meant to be at work."

"That's an exaggeration. Also, I've done ten times as much work as you have."

"You're not corporeally challenged!"

Jia burst out laughing. "That's a new one."

"Oh, now you're ganging up on me." Mart huffed.

"You tried to make me look bad, so fair's fair." I left him grumbling behind the bar, while I went to ask Allie's permission to go to talk to Drew and help with the next stage of the investigation.

———

On my way to meet Drew, I stopped by the witches' headquarters again. The windows were tinted so I couldn't see any signs of ingredient stores inside. While the door wasn't locked, it made such a loud creaking noise that I instinctively dropped the handle. On my second attempt, a raging shock travelled up my arm, and I let go with a hiss of pain. Had they booby-trapped the door?

"What are you doing here?"

I spun around. A woman dressed in bright-pink attire

crossed the road to accost me. I recognised her from the sole coven meeting I'd attended as one of the people who'd supported Mina Devlin. What was her name, Marie?

"I'm looking for someone who can help me buy herbs." I tucked my throbbing hand under my arm. "I noticed the apothecary is closed, and someone seems to have accidentally put a shocking charm on the door."

"You'll have to look elsewhere," she told me. "The coven headquarters is only open to members."

"It wasn't, the last time I checked the rules." Drew ought to back me up on that, but he had better things to do than mediate an agreement with one of Mina's former cronies. "Haven't you found a replacement for Angie yet?"

"That's none of your business, since she died because of you."

So much for avoiding an argument, but that comment was way out of line. "She died because her own coven leader betrayed her."

Her eyes narrowed. "You enjoy twisting the facts, don't you?"

"I seem to remember your former coven leader liked twisting the facts so much that she made a career out of it. Then she fled town rather than admit to being wrong."

"I suppose that Jia is spreading her own lies too," she spat. "You're as bad as each other."

"That wasn't the insult you thought it was, trust me." I walked away from her at a fast stride and was relieved to see Drew waiting outside the police station.

Drew waved at me as I crossed the road. "What is it? You look like you're about to use your Reaper skills on someone."

"The witches," I growled under my breath. "I went to see if I could borrow some ingredients for a summoning spell, and one of Mina's cronies ambushed me. She claimed non-coven members aren't allowed into their headquarters and accused me of spreading lies about her beloved leader."

"I can set her straight on that."

"Never mind her. I'm just frustrated that the coven's still supporting Mina. You'd think her penchant for covering up murders and worse would be a deal breaker."

"Worse?"

Ah. I hadn't told him she might have caused the flood which had killed countless people and buried half the town underwater twenty-odd years ago, but now wasn't the time for that conversation.

"Yeah, the coven's karaoke nights were worse than murder. Even the ghosts avoided them."

"That sounds like a wise decision to me."

If he'd suspected a diversion, he didn't say. With the witches still taking Mina's side over mine and Mina Devlin at large, it seemed a risky time to stoke that particular fire.

Maybe Jia was right, and we'd all be better off if we tracked Mina down and brought her to account for her crimes, but that was a matter to deal with when we didn't have any urgent werewolf murders to solve.

"Anyway, what's the verdict on the cause of death?" I asked Drew.

"Poison, as I expected," he said. "The family begrudgingly allowed us to examine the body, and we found traces of hemlock leaves on him. Deadly poison, and easy enough for a werewolf or shifter with little knowledge of the subject to use to kill someone."

"You talked to his parents?"

He inclined his head. "They're not up for receiving visitors, but they begrudgingly agreed to speak to me. I have yet to speak to his brother, though. The two were close, so if his ghost picked anyone to haunt, I imagine it'd be him."

"Doing a summoning spell is off the table as long as I can't get the ingredients." Assuming it would even work when it'd been more than a day since his death. "You still want me to come, though?"

"I'd like that, yes."

Warmth filled my chest despite my suspicion that I'd be little help in the investigation without being able to speak to Davey's ghost. If Drew wanted my company, who was I to say no?

My first regret came when we reached the park. Several shifters roamed the paths, and all of them turned to stare as we passed by. Whispers followed in their wake. *Reaper.*

"Word spreads fast, doesn't it?" I said to Drew in an undertone.

"Ignore them," he told me. "Shana was a little too talkative about yesterday at a pack event last night."

"So everyone knows the Reaper has been here." Pity I hadn't done much Reaper-ing. In any case, I stared right back at them until we reached the exit and headed into a cul-de-sac on the west side of the park.

From there, Drew led me to two adjoined houses at the end of the road. "Davey lived here next door to his brother, Lewis. See any ghosts?"

I scanned the area. "Not here. Hang on a second."

Shadows extended from my hands, but I'd barely got a grip on them before they slipped away. Weird. I tried again, peering into the darkness, but I'd seen enough to know there weren't any ghosts around.

"No luck?" he asked.

I shook my head, mildly unnerved. "Nope. Are you sure it's a good idea for me to be here?"

"Of course." His hand brushed mine in reassurance. "You have every right to be here."

He knocked on the door of the house on the right-hand side. A broad werewolf with darker hair than was typical of the local shifters answered. "Detective."

His voice was husky and his eyes red around the edges, a more obvious display of grief than any of Davey's family members, though perhaps that was to be expected.

"Lewis, I'm sorry for your loss," Drew said. "May I come in?"

"You know the cause of death," he croaked. "What more do you want?"

"To know if you have any information which might help us bring your brother's killer to justice." Drew spoke in a gentle tone of voice. "Maura is here to back me up."

A growling note entered his tone. "Come to Reap my brother's ghost, has she?"

Pretty sure he already did that to himself. "No. It's usually easier to find a murderer if the victim himself gives evidence. May I look around while Drew asks some questions?"

He blinked. "Reapers help solve crimes now?"

"I do, yes." It wasn't even a lie.

His gaze lingered on Drew, then his shoulders sagged. "Fine, fine. Come in."

I'd officially confused him into letting us in without asking questions. Go me. In fairness, most shifters rarely got offers from the local Reaper to search their homes for ghosts, nor did they have any particular reason to think about the subject at all.

Lewis's property was far smaller than the chief's home, more of a bachelor pad. The mud all over the hall, hair on the furniture and a stack of unwashed dishes in the kitchen gave an air of someone who didn't often entertain guests, and I had to move a pile of video games out of the way to make room for Drew and me to sit down on the sofa.

"Go on." Lewis addressed Drew. "What do you want to know?"

"When was the last time you saw your brother?" Drew asked. "Your parents said you saw him the morning of his death."

"He dropped by to borrow his spare key."

"You have a key to his property," said Drew. "Have you been into his house lately?"

"I keep a spare key in case he loses his own, which happens a lot. Why?"

"I searched the house yesterday and found no signs of a break-in," Drew told him. "If someone caught him unawares at home, might they have borrowed your key to get in?"

"I thought he was murdered at the park."

"That's where we found him, but in my experience, it's hard to ambush a werewolf while they're awake. The person who poisoned him must have exercised extreme stealth if they sneaked up on him in the open."

Good point. I'd been thinking of motives, but Drew was the one with the details of who might have conceivably been able to ambush and kill a werewolf without him sinking his teeth into them. If Davey hadn't been asleep at home, how had the murderer taken him by surprise?

Lewis blinked. "You're the detective, not me. If his ghost can't tell you the truth, then I sure as hell can't."

I didn't see any signs of his brother's ghost in the house, but I hadn't really expected to. After all, the house was close enough to the park that I'd have sensed him the previous day if he'd been here. Unfortunately, no ghosts would step in to help me with this one.

"Putting aside the odd circumstances," Drew began, "I'm told not everyone in your family was thrilled by his decision to marry Shana."

"I think it's absurd for them to assume they were uniting the pack," he scoffed. "As if a simple marriage would solve years of rivalries."

"Her sister would agree with you there," I told him. "She objected for the same reasons. But Shana was adamant, as were her parents."

"Don't I know it. The pack chief's word is law, and his daughter charmed my brother's wits straight out of him."

I'd heard something similar from Tessa too. "So you think he did want to marry Shana, but not everyone agreed. Would anyone have taken extreme measures to stop the wedding?"

"Evidently someone did," he growled. "The chief's people have been sniffing around here for the past day, but if they couldn't find answers, I doubt you will, Reaper."

"Did you know of the marriage arrangement before it took place?" Drew asked. "Is it common for the chief to reach out to rivals?"

"No," he said. "Pack marriages aren't as popular as some people think they are. Davey only agreed because he fell head over heels for that girl, and she wanted out of her parents' house."

That fit with what I'd heard from her sister too. "They were completely on board with it? What about your parents?"

"They tried to talk sense into him, but he wasn't having any of it." He pulled a face. "Typical of him. Wanted to do his own thing. Like you, Detective. If you wanted to set the rumour mill spinning, you definitely succeeded when you brought your Reaper witch girl-friend to talk to the chief."

"I'm sorry, what?" Since when was it any of his busi-ness? It was also the first time I'd heard myself referred to using the word *girlfriend*, but I'd rather have heard it from Drew himself than from a guy who couldn't even seem to do his own dishes.

"Maura has nothing to do with your grievances with the chief," said Drew.

"She does if she's going to get involved with you." Lewis's mouth turned down at the corners. "You annoyed a lot of people when you took her to visit the chief."

"I wasn't aware you spoke for everyone in the pack." I managed to rein in my temper, with difficulty. "The chief's daughter gave me permission to contact your brother's ghost, if you want to be pedantic, and then her father insisted on asking me questions. I seem to remember your family was refusing visitors at the time."

Drew cleared his throat. "Lewis, it's my job to speak to anyone who has information to give me. Putting aside her father, what did you think of Shana?"

"She's fickle, spoiled, and melodramatic." He listed the words off on his fingers. "I also thought she was going to marry Ian Tanner if she picked anyone."

"Who's that?" I asked.

"They were childhood friends," said Lewis. "They had a fling when they were teenagers. Davey was obsessed with her even then, but he didn't have the courage to approach her."

"Then why would she have changed her mind?" asked Drew.

"Like I said, she's fickle. Also, her family wanted her off their hands. If they could marry her into a good family to strengthen pack relations, so much the better. Their oldest daughter already left and for good reason."

True, but I'd sooner eat my wand than admit I agreed with him. "She's still at university, though. Don't they want her to have the chance to make something of her own life first?"

Lewis gave a derisive laugh. "What use is a degree in arts? That won't get her a job with the pack. I can see why they tried marrying her off instead."

"Harsh." Was Davey's family better off financially than this Ian Tanner person? It was beyond my ability to tell, and besides, we had no proof of her alleged former interest in Ian except Lewis's word. "Did you know her well, then?"

"No, but everyone knows everyone else's business here," said Lewis. "Part of being in the pack."

If that was a subtle dig at me for not being one of the shifters, I didn't appreciate it.

"Is there anything else you want to tell us?" Drew asked. "Who else might have had a reason to target your brother?"

He exhaled in a sigh. "I don't know, but he didn't deserve what they did to him. And I wish I could find the culprit."

"It's my intention to do exactly that," said Drew. "Thank you for your time."

We left the house, and Lewis wasted no time in closing the door on our heels.

"Good riddance," I muttered. "I wasn't aware that the pack had such a large stake in your romantic life."

"Ignore him," said Drew. "He's angry and grieving, and he's right that Davey's friends wouldn't have been thrilled that I took you to see the chief. I didn't think of that before."

"The chief is in charge of the pack, though." I did my best to ignore the sting. "Putting his family's connection to the victim aside, surely it's hard to solve a case like this one *without* talking to the chief."

"The others don't necessarily see it that way," he said. "In any case, they're only looking out for the pack."

"I'm less than convinced they're all looking out for the *same* pack."

"You probably aren't wrong there, but I doubt they want to hear it."

I grimaced. "I know, I shouldn't have spoken to him like that, but he was rubbing me up the wrong way.

Maybe I shouldn't have come. It's not as if my ghost-hunting skills have been much help, and I seem to tick the werewolves off without even trying."

"Don't sell yourself short," he said. "Even when you're not ghost hunting, you sometimes think of questions which don't occur to me when questioning suspects. You think outside the box."

"Hazard of being unable to fit into any box myself." I smiled despite myself. "But thanks. What now, then? I can go back to the inn, but it seems a waste to come all the way here without annoying a few more people."

"I planned to talk to this Ian Tanner person next."

"You mean the guy Shana supposedly had a fling with?" I considered this. "In case she secretly had an affair going on with him or something?"

"It's certainly plausible," he said. "I think we should talk to him and see if he can shed any light on the situation."

7

To start off with, Drew needed to get Ian's address, so I had to choose between accompanying him to the police station or doing something useful of my own. I hadn't seen Davey's ghost at his brother's house, so only one option remained… getting the ingredients for a witch-style summoning. And while Marie had done her best to put me off going into the coven's headquarters, I knew for a fact that all the necessary ingredients were in there.

I also knew it wasn't locked, despite the spell they'd put on the door.

Drew didn't try to dissuade me from my plan when we parted ways outside the police station, though I'd freely admit it wasn't my best one. Short of knocking on every witch's door and asking to borrow their supplies, though, I was out of any better ideas.

Upon reaching the witches' headquarters, I considered the bronze unicorns and griffins on the exterior, trying to see if there were any side entrances which would enable me to get in without tripping any alarms. None leapt out at me, and besides, I wouldn't have put it past Mina's cronies to have put a security spell on the entire building, especially after my visit earlier that day.

Time to go with the Reaper approach, then.

Shadows swept around me, masking the door. In one smooth motion, I stepped through the shadows, envisioning Mina Devlin's office in my mind's eye.

Instead, my head struck a hard surface, causing stars to wink before my eyes. The shadows pulled back, revealing the outside of the witches' headquarters. I hadn't got past the door? Seriously?

I took a step back, rubbing my forehead, then called the shadows back. It took a fair bit more effort than it should have, but soon enough, darkness covered the bronze statues and magenta-painted walls. *Let's try this again.*

I pictured the interior of Mina Devlin's office and took a determined step forward into the darkness, only to collide with an invisible barrier. Or rather, the front door of the building. Fool me twice, shame on me. I knew when I was beaten, so I gathered the last shreds of my dignity and set about entering the building the normal way instead.

I pulled out my wand and cast a negation spell which ought to counter any nasty tripwire spells on the door. Then I cast an *unseen* spell on myself that would make anyone who looked in my direction overlook my presence unless I intentionally drew their attention.

That would have to do, so I opened the door with one hand. Aside from a slight tingle of static, no shock hit me this time. Closing it behind me as quietly as I could manage, I scanned the lobby in search of the storeroom. Nobody was around, so I crossed the carpeted floor and examined each door until I found one surrounded by the promising smell of herbs. I tried the handle. Locked, as I'd suspected.

I pulled my wand out to use an unlocking charm, and the sound of footsteps on the stairs made my heart sink in my chest. Uh-oh.

"There she is." Marie came puffing into the lobby and jabbed a triumphant finger in my direction.

Behind her, her friend Angela, along with several other brightly dressed witches, descended into the lobby. I must have somehow alerted their attention when I'd come in, and if they already knew I was here, then no *unseen* spell would mask me from sight.

I held up my hands in surrender, but I didn't dare put down my wand either. "Wait a second. There's been a misunderstanding."

"How dare you sneak into our headquarters," Angela said. "Disgraceful."

"I wouldn't have needed to sneak around if you hadn't acted like I was trespassing by walking in front of the building." I addressed Marie.

She raised her wand. "Would you be as keen to break into our storeroom if I turned you into a broomstick?"

"Surely you can think of something more imaginative than that."

Time to go. While I had zero desire to walk into any walls in front of an audience, my Reaper skills were the quickest way out. As Marie raised her wand, shadows folded around me, smothering my surroundings. I stepped forward, only for the darkness to wink out like a light switch had been turned on in a pitch-black room. *Huh?*

What was going on? It wasn't like I was trying to get to an unknown location, so there was no reason whatsoever for my shadowy powers not to work.

Angela laughed. "Was that supposed to be scary?"

The front door opened with such a loud crash that all eyes instantly turned in that direction. Relief swept through me when Drew walked in, his gaze roving over the gathering witches. "Is there a problem?"

"She's trespassing!" Marie objected.

"I'm not trespassing. I'm trying to get some ingredients from the storeroom." He already knew, so I mostly spoke for the benefit of the other witches who'd gone along with Marie's plan. "The law states that any witch or wizard can borrow supplies if none are available elsewhere."

"Precisely," said Drew. "The coven headquarters is open to all witches and wizards."

"She's not a witch, she's a Reaper," Marie argued. "And she's not part of our coven."

"Last I heard, there *was* no coven, unless you elected a new leader since I last asked." His smooth tone dared them to contradict him. "Since no official coven owns the building, Maura has every right to be here."

Thanks, Drew. I hadn't known the witches had officially disbanded the coven, but he knew the rule book better than I did and had the clout to back it up.

"Mina Devlin owns the building," Angela said. "Someone might have run her out of town, but it's still hers."

"She's a wanted criminal." I nodded to Drew. "She's not coming back."

Marie's wand jerked in her hand. "She's worth twelve of you and your traitorous new co-worker."

Drew cleared his throat. "Mina Devlin *is* wanted for questioning by the police, and I would appreciate it if you let Maura access your storeroom."

"What does she even want from the storeroom?" asked Angela.

"Drew, never mind." I turned my back on the witches. "I'll have to look elsewhere for the ingredients I need to help you with your investigation."

Marie frowned. "Investigation?"

A few murmurs of interest passed between the witches.

A middle-aged witch with mauve hair that clashed with her green attire addressed Drew. "If *you* wanted the ingredients, why send her instead of coming here yourself?"

"Maura is a witch," Drew told them. "Besides, it happens that I'm investigating a murder which may have been committed using certain herbs that were acquired from your stores."

Wait, what? I'd thought he'd already come to the conclusion that the werewolves had poisoned Davey without needing to acquire any rare ingredients, but the witches didn't need to know. They all wore scandalised expressions at his proclamation.

"Are you accusing us of abetting a murderer?" Marie queried. "Because I don't appreciate that."

"I'm not accusing anyone of anything, but I would appreciate it if you stopped threatening my girlfriend."

I definitely liked the word a lot more coming from him, despite the circumstances. If my Reaper skills had been working, I could have given them a real scare, but I wasn't up for another round of humiliation.

"You're supposed to be impartial," Angela argued. "You're the chief of police, aren't you?"

"I'm also the lead detective on a murder case," he said. "May I access your supplies?"

Marie lowered her wand. "What do you need?"

"The herbs necessary to summon a ghost."

Maria and Angela exchanged bewildered glances.

"I thought she didn't need them." The mauve-haired witch indicated me. "She's a Reaper."

Had the entire town been debating my Reaper status in recent weeks? "Can you just tell me whether you have the ingredients or not? I hardly think you must make a habit of summoning ghosts on a regular basis."

"We don't have them," Marie replied. "Our coven supplier cut us off when Mina left town."

"Exactly," Angela put in. "Nobody will deal with us now that we're no longer an official coven, and it's all thanks to you."

"Is that so?" Drew didn't sound convinced. "You'd better be telling the truth."

I wasn't sure on that one either, but I'd lost all interest in the idea of attempting a last-ditch ghost summoning. "Word of advice? You might get more covens willing to trade with you if you didn't booby-trap your doors."

And with that, Drew and I left the witches' headquarters. Part of me expected one of the witches to fling a hex at me from behind, but they managed to restrain themselves. Good, because I wasn't in the mood for a fight.

"Somehow, I don't think I'll be invited to the next coven party." The door swung closed behind us. "Did you get this Ian Tanner person's address? I know I should be heading back to the inn soon…"

"Ian works at a newsagents' just around the corner from here, so we can stop by on the way back," he said. "Are you sure you're okay? You have a bruise on your forehead."

"I walked into the door." Heat crept up my neck. "I tried to use my Reaper skills to get into the witches' headquarters. Twice, because apparently I didn't learn my lesson the first time around."

"Really?" His eyes widened a little. "Did they do something to the building to ward it against Reapers?"

"I didn't think it was possible to keep Reapers out with a simple warding spell," I admitted. "We can walk through most protective spells without being affected in the slightest."

My failure to use my Reaper skills to get into the witches' headquarters bothered me more than not being able to find Davey's ghost because I had no explanation whatsoever. Had they truly warded the place against me, or was the problem on my end?

"Never mind that," I added. "I can't believe the coven just… fell apart."

"Mina Devlin must have planned to have no opposition to her leadership, so it's no surprise that they've struggled in her absence." Drew accepted my change of subject without a fuss, to my relief. "It's as if they're waiting for her return, which is troubling."

"Tell me about it," I murmured. "You *are* looking for her, right? The police, I mean?"

"Our options are limited, unfortunately. Finding a witch who doesn't want to be found would be tricky even if she'd remained in the area, and there's no guarantee that she has."

I thought back to Jia's eagerness to find her. Would some of the other witches she'd driven out of town be keen to see her brought to justice too? "Can't you at least put someone else in charge of the coven so they can get back to being semi-functioning?"

"The witches would never allow a shifter to appoint someone else on their behalf, and the police have little recourse to get involved when no obvious crime has been committed."

"Apart from booby-trapping their headquarters." Would they all support Mina if I told the entire town that she might have been the one who flooded the town twenty years ago? Nobody would take my word for it without proof, of course. Not without an outright confession from Mina herself, and considering my Reaper powers had been acting up, I'd better hope she waited a long while before returning to confront me again.

In the meantime, Drew led the way across the street towards a newsagent and pushed the door inward. The red-haired shifter behind the counter looked up sharply when we entered. He must be Ian Tanner.

"Detective," he said in the growling voice I'd come to associate with male shifters. "Heard you were doing the rounds among the pack members."

"Then you know why I'm here?"

Hope he has a plan. I hadn't the faintest clue how to delicately ask if Ian had been having an affair with Shana before her fiancé's untimely death, but that was Drew's job, not mine.

The werewolf eyed me. "Is she the Reaper Witch?"

I should have figured he'd have heard about me too. "I'm here to assist Drew, nothing more."

"You want to know when I last saw Davey," he said. "I suppose you heard he came here to buy a few things the morning of his death."

"No." Drew's voice was tinged with surprise. "I *did* hear that you might have once wanted to marry Shana."

His brows shot up. "Huh? Who told you that?"

"That's between me and them, I'm afraid," Drew replied. "You knew Shana when you were teenagers."

"Did the *chief* tell you that?" he growled. "Typical of him. He can't stand the notion of someone in the pack killing his daughter's fiancé, so he's got his lackeys doing their best to place the blame with Davey's own friends and acquaintances instead."

Really? I hadn't known the pack chief had been spreading some of the rumours himself, but if someone from among his rivals had killed one of their own to prevent a union with the chief's family, that spelled trouble for the entire pack.

"No, it wasn't the chief who told me," said Drew. "However, it's not a big secret that you and Shana were acquainted as children, and if you were seeing one another more recently, then it might be relevant."

Ian scoffed. "Do you think I'd risk ticking off the chief? I'd be run out of town."

"If you saw Davey here the day of his death, did he say anything to you?" asked Drew.

"Huh?" He blinked. "Not that I remember. He bought a paper and a lottery ticket, that's all. And a pack of chewing gum."

"Thank you for talking to us," Drew said. "We'll leave you in peace now."

Strange. Had Lewis tried to send us in the wrong direction on purpose? Or did he just want to avoid directing blame at the chief's own family?

Drew let the shop door swing closed behind us. "At least we've ticked one potential suspect off the list."

"Any more ideas?" I was late returning to the inn, I knew, but I couldn't help wondering how Davey had gone from buying gum from the newsagent to dead in the park in the space of a few hours with nobody knowing how he'd got there.

"Not yet. Want me to walk with you back to the inn?"

"Guess so." We crossed the road and made our way past the witches' headquarters again. "I can't say anyone we've spoken to has given me cause to suspect them, but Lewis must have known he was sending us in the wrong direction."

"Not necessarily," he said. "Ian's the first person who's admitted to seeing Davey on the day of his death, if nothing else."

"But we have no obvious clues pointing to the culprit, do we? Most of the pack is still on the suspect list."

"They chose poisoning as their method," Drew said, "which implies that they wanted to throw suspicion off the werewolves in general, but it also makes it more likely that one of them did it. It also indicates that his murder was planned ahead of time rather than an act of passion in the heat of the moment, but without any witnesses, we can't be sure."

"Weren't there any?" My mind drifted back to Belinda Jennings. I wouldn't be inclined to take her word for anything at all, but she *had* been there at the scene of the crime. Whether she'd witnessed anything she could recount to the rest of us, though, was debatable. "Not to the actual murder, but you'd think someone at the park saw them disposing of the body."

"So far nobody has come forward."

"They must have carried the body themselves, since they can't have used magic. Hauling a dead body around isn't what I'd call subtle."

"They might have used a body bag or something similar," Drew reminded me. "There are routes through the park which make it possible to avoid prying eyes too."

There was a small chance that one of the shifters who'd found Davey's body had actually been responsible for putting it there, but as far as impartial witnesses went, I could only think of one person. "Drew, remember that wannabe Seer I mentioned? She might have seen the killer."

"Her?" His brow furrowed. "I don't think she's a reliable witness, Maura."

"Nor I, but who else was wandering around the park at that time who had nothing to do with the pack?"

Admittedly, she probably wouldn't have recognised a potential murderer even if they'd been right in front of her nose, but that didn't mean questioning her more closely wouldn't shake a clue or two loose.

"You think she might have seen the killer?"

"There's a chance." A small one, I'd freely admit. "If she saw a bunch of people carrying a body bag, I think that would have stuck in her mind."

"Do you know where she lives?"

"No, but I saw her hanging around the witches' headquarters." She'd been inside, in fact, despite not being part of the coven. If anything, that further disproved Marie's claims that non-coven witches weren't allowed to enter. "My new co-worker also ran into her in a field when she flew into town. Not sure if she was stargazing again, since it was daytime, but who knows."

"You're not selling this to me, Maura."

"Believe me, I'm not selling it to myself either." We were scraping at the bottom of the barrel if we hoped to get any useful information whatsoever from Belinda Jennings, but Drew was far better at questioning people than I was, shifters or otherwise. Maybe he'd be able to probe her memory and dredge up something of use.

8

The universe had other ideas. Belinda might be in any number of places, but I opted to start with the first place I'd seen her. It wouldn't hurt to have another look at the place where Davey's body had originally shown up too. Drew and I backtracked down the high street towards the werewolves' park, where he kept an eye out for potential interruptions, while I went in search of our elusive would-be Seer.

The bushes were dense and the trees close enough that it wouldn't have been impossible for someone to carry a body bag around without tipping off any nearby shifters, especially when it was growing dark. If Belinda had been in the bushes at the time, though, they might have veered right next to her hiding place without knowing she was there.

I came to a sudden halt when my feet caught on a familiar pair of binoculars lying on the edge of the path. Had she dropped them? "Drew, look over here."

He turned around with a questioning look on his face. I picked up the binoculars and then scanned the bushes for their owner. A glint caught my eye, and I skirted the bushes into a clearing. A chill raced over my skin. "Drew, you might want to look over here."

Belinda Jennings lay half in and half out of the bushes, her eyes closed. Drew trod over to her, his steps almost silent. "No wounds," he murmured. "She wasn't attacked."

"But she's dead, right?" I gingerly approached her body, while Drew crouched in the bushes. "I didn't sense her die."

Not that it mattered to poor Belinda, but this was the second time in a week I hadn't sensed someone's death. *What is wrong with my Reaper powers?*

My phone buzzed in my pocket. "Ah, I think Allie wants to know where I am."

"Let me handle this." Drew pulled out his own phone to call for backup.

"Allie." I answered the call and took a step back from the clearing. "Sorry, we found another body in the park. I might be back a little late."

My free hand clenched over Belinda's binoculars, which I'd forgotten I was holding. Their location suggested that her killer had struck right here in the park, but there were no visible wounds on her body, and if she'd died by poison like Davey had... well, she was easier to sneak up on than a shifter, but the odds were just as strong that the killer had purposefully thrown the binoculars onto the path to lead us to the body.

My mind whirled, and I hardly heard Allie's response through the phone. Had Belinda seen the killer the other night? Maybe the murderer had the same thought as I had, and when Belinda had returned right here to the scene of the crime, they'd decided to remove the one possible witness. They might have hunted her down somewhere else and brought her body here—but why? To frame the pack? To sow discord, as if there wasn't plenty of that already?

Whatever the case, she must have seen something that evening. It was the only explanation that made sense. Too bad I'd never be able to ask her for the details.

Unless I called her ghost.

I ended the call, my pulse fluttering with nerves. This was ridiculous. I shouldn't be afraid to use my own powers thanks to some cowardly prank the witches had played on me.

Sternly telling myself to get a grip, I turned on my Reaper senses, calling the shadows towards me. Then I peered into the darkness in search of a spark of light.

None appeared, while the shadows collapsed an instant later. Teeth clenched, I did the same again.

"Belinda," I called into the shadows. "Belinda Jennings."

No response. I couldn't sense her ghost at all. I let the shadows drop, my heart swooping when I saw that several shifters gathered on both sides of the path, murmuring among themselves. I caught the word *Reaper* several times.

Ignoring them, I trod over to Drew. "I can't find her. Belinda's ghost isn't around."

I didn't give him any details, since I didn't need half the pack to know the earlier problems that I'd had with my Reaper powers. Drew gave a nod and then faced the oncoming shifters. "Did any of you see this woman earlier today?"

"What's a witch doing in our park?" one of them growled. "She shouldn't be here."

"It's not forbidden for non-shifters to come into the park," said Drew. "More to the point, she's dead. Someone left her body in the bushes over there."

An angry rumble travelled through the werewolves. One spoke. "The witches. They put her body here to frame us."

"The *witches?*" I regretted my outburst when all their attention turned on me. "From the looks of things, she was poisoned the same way Davey Rogers was."

More growling ensued, but Drew's voice cut through their anger. "We believe the killer might be the same individual. If anyone has any information to give me, I'd greatly appreciate it if you stepped forward."

"She was a witness to the first murder," I added. "She might have seen who killed Davey."

"Then why didn't you question her sooner?" someone demanded.

"We were on our way to do exactly that when we found her," Drew told them. "I suspect she was targeted for the same reason."

The shifters' growls drowned out the end of his sentence. Half the pack was here, and while I didn't see the chief, I did recognise his daughter among them. Shana's flinty eyes found mine, accusing, as if to say, *You failed to find my future husband's killer, and now another person is dead.*

What a waste. Killing Belinda might not have been necessary at all, given her lack of attention to the real world, but if the person responsible had wanted to rile up the pack even further, they'd succeeded. Growls rippled through the crowd, while our only escape route was to shove our way through angry werewolves on the verge of shifting and tearing one another to pieces.

"This wouldn't have happened if your father didn't let outsiders roam around our territory," someone growled at Shana.

"Don't you dare blame the chief," she snarled back. "Would you dare to say that to his face, I wonder?"

"He let the detective bring that human with him, too, so it's no surprise he refuses to listen," another werewolf put in. "Yet he has the nerve to accuse *us* of stirring up trouble when someone killed one of our own."

Reading between the lines, he must be an acquaintance of Davey, which meant the crowd consisted of a mixture of both of the pack's two factions. In other words, I needed to make a quick getaway before fur started flying and teeth started biting. Too bad my glitchy Reaper skills had marooned me here next to Drew and the body of a witch who they'd all but forgotten already. Annoyance on her behalf rose to the forefront of my thoughts. The whole reason I'd ended up entrenched in this was because I'd wanted to find Davey's ghost.

"A human is dead on your territory." I raised my voice to cut through the growling. "Maybe focus on that and not your personal grievances?"

"A witch," Shana corrected. "And she shouldn't have been here to begin with."

"Maybe that was what the killer wanted you to think."

Honestly. They seemed more annoyed about a witch trespassing in their park than about the fact that someone had murdered her. Nobody had even brought up the possibility of the coven raising a fuss over her body being found on their territory… probably because the coven had no leader and Belinda hadn't even been a member.

Still, I might as well have tried to negotiate over broomstick parking spaces with a pigeon. Would the werewolves even order an investigation into her death? I had my doubts, but the coven certainly wouldn't either, which meant that the task would likely fall onto Drew's head instead. Just perfect.

Shana stalked over to Drew and me. "Isn't the Reaper going to make herself useful and find her ghost?"

"Her ghost isn't around," I answered.

"How convenient." She scoffed at Drew. "If you ask me, this was an excuse for you to bring that girlfriend of yours here and flaunt her in front of the pack."

"That's what you think?" I might have failed to find the ghost, but I was getting sick of being dismissed as an outsider on principle. "Give me a break. Drew doesn't need to use me to impress the likes of you."

"Then it's clear he's chosen you over the pack."

"That's enough." A growl underlaid Drew's voice. "Maura is here to assist me, and I'd appreciate it if you respected her."

"Respect must be earned."

"Speak for yourself." Maybe it was the shifter-laden tension in the air, but I kind of wanted to throw a punch at her. If my shadows had been in full working order, I might have tried it just to see her expression, but I didn't need to join Belinda's body in the bushes.

Shana straightened upright, her gaze catching on something behind us. "Finally. My father is here."

Sure enough, the imposing figure of the chief came into view. At once, the werewolves converged on him in a chorus of growls. They'd also left an escape route, which was our cue to leave.

Drew edged closer to me. "I don't think this is going to be resolved anytime soon. You should get back to the inn."

"I don't want them attacking you because of me." They'd all liked and respected Drew as recently as a few days ago. The murder hadn't helped, but I couldn't shake the feeling that I'd unintentionally turned half the pack against him simply by stepping onto shifter territory.

"It's not you." He leaned in to murmur the words into my ear, eliciting a rush of warmth when his lips brushed my ear. "I'll text you when I have an update, okay?"

"Sure." I turned away, trying to ignore the sinking feeling in my chest.

It didn't matter if the pack respected me or not. I was with Drew, and they'd have to deal with it.

"I can't let you go anywhere, can I?" Mart shook his head at me. "Right, that does it. From now on, I'll be your shadow."

"Please don't," I said. "I'm pretty sure I'm not going to be helping out the detective any longer, besides."

Okay, Drew hadn't said so himself, but I'd returned to the inn more or less in disgrace after my total failure at the park. Allie had been understanding once I'd explained that the killer had claimed a second victim, but a Reaper who couldn't speak to ghosts wasn't much of a Reaper at all.

I'd waited until Mart and I were alone in my room before I'd explained the real depths of the trouble that I'd landed in.

"At least you won't miss any more work shifts," Mart said. "Is that an upside? I think it is."

"I should have questioned her before." I sank onto the bed and rested my head in my hands. "Why didn't I try harder? I'm sure she must have seen something useful in the park, even if she didn't recognise it at the time."

"From what you've said, she's about as much use as a broomstick made of paper. Stop beating yourself up."

"My Reaper powers aren't much use either," I mumbled into my hands. "I couldn't even shadow-walk into the witches' headquarters earlier."

"What did you want to do that for?"

"To get some ingredients to summon a ghost." I lifted my head. "Mina Devlin's cronies booby-trapped the door, but that's not why I couldn't walk through it. Anyway, they claimed they aren't getting deliveries anymore."

"So you annoyed the witches as well as the shifters? That's twice the reason for me to keep you out of trouble."

"Hey, it's not just me they're mad at," I protested. "They're not best pleased with Drew, either. He tried to leverage the investigation as an excuse to get into their supplies, but they weren't having any of it. Besides, we wouldn't have needed to sneak into their storeroom if they hadn't shut down the apothecary, so the only place to get hold of any ingredients is their own base."

"That's dodgy, that is. Don't they want any non-coven members to be able to brew up potions?"

"Probably not."

"Tell Jia, then. Bet she'll help you *borrow* some supplies if you ask her nicely."

"No use if there's nothing to steal." I shrugged. "Mina seems to have left the place in complete anarchy, and Drew can't police the coven as well as wrangling shifters. I have no idea what Mina and the others will make of Belinda's death."

Since she wasn't a coven member, they likely wouldn't be bothered, but Drew had more than enough to handle already, what with the werewolf pack on the brink of tearing itself apart.

"What did the wolves think, then?" Mart asked.

"They were more annoyed that Belinda was on their territory when she died than the fact that she was, you know, dead." I heaved a sigh. "I might have mitigated the situation if I'd been able to find her ghost, but no luck."

"Should I fetch some other ghosts for you to practise on?"

"Look, I don't want the whole world to know my Reaper powers are acting up. I just wish I knew why it was happening. Do you think I should check with the Reaper?"

"If it sets your mind at ease?" he said. "Absolutely."

I blinked at him. "I think that's the first time you've given the thumbs-up to my suggestion of talking to Harold."

"I don't think it's a good idea," he added. "But it's hardly worse than poking around the shifters when they're in a temper."

Fair point. I'd have to go before my shift started tomorrow, which shouldn't be an issue. I wouldn't be helping Drew question anyone else, given that the pack clearly didn't want me around and the lack of any functioning Reaper skills made it hard for me to justify riling them up any further.

Still, I'd get answers, even if it meant throwing myself on the mercy of the notoriously grumpy retired Reaper.

9

The following morning, I set off to see the Reaper. Since Allie wasn't in the reception area and Carey hadn't come downstairs yet, I walked out of the inn's automatic doors without being seen by anyone.

Mart floated alongside me, yawning theatrically as I crossed the bridge over the river. "It's too early for me."

"You don't even sleep."

"Watching you toss and turn gave me second-hand tiredness."

"That's not a thing." I gave up arguing with him, though, deciding to save my energy for Harold the Reaper instead. The town's cemetery wasn't typically somewhere I spent a lot of time, since the town's ghostly inhabitants tended to congregate elsewhere, and everyone avoided the place except its sole living occupant. Harold the Reaper wasn't exactly a social butterfly. More of an anti-social moth. After the floods had claimed the life of his former apprentice, he'd spent the past two decades sitting in solitude and letting the town become overrun with ghosts.

I'd never exactly intended to become his replacement, especially as the Reaper Council would technically categorise me as a rogue after I'd quit my apprenticeship, but I'd got into the habit of using my skills when I needed to, and the notion of losing my powers didn't sit right with me.

I walked to the cottage—numbered forty-two for no reason I could figure out, since Harold had never admitted to being a *Hitchhiker's Guide to the Galaxy* fan and had no sense of humour besides—and knocked on the wooden door.

"Go away," he said, right on cue.

"I wanted to ask you a question about my Reaper powers."

"If you want me to help you adopt another ghost you feel sorry for, you're out of luck."

"No." I ignored his derisive tone. "Two people have died in the last week, and I didn't sense their deaths. Did you?"

"I'm retired," he growled. "I don't keep tabs on dead people. I'd never get a moment's peace if I did."

"You get nothing *but* peace out here," I pointed out. "Besides, I wouldn't come here if this wasn't an emergency. Can a Reaper lose their powers?"

"If anyone can, it's you."

What? "I want a serious answer, Harold."

"That *is* the serious answer," he said. "Can an active Reaper lose their powers? Generally, no. An inactive one, though... that's a different question and one I'm sure you already know the answer to."

Meaning it's true. "I tried to shadow-walk earlier, and that didn't work either."

"If you're looking for sympathy, you're out of luck," he growled. "So are the ghosts, come to that."

"The problem is that there *aren't* ghosts of the two people who died in the past week, and the shifter pack is on the brink of starting a war over it."

"That is none of my business," he said. "Or yours either."

"Like the coven?"

"Like the coven."

Anger flooded my veins. The coven's actions had led to his apprentice's death, so you'd think he'd show a little more spine. "Even if they crossed the Reaper Council?"

His door jerked open a fraction, and his angry face appeared in the gap. "I'd advise you to leave the coven *and* the Council alone, unless you want me to turn you in. You forget I already covered for you once."

So he planned on holding that against me forever, did he? The bloody Reaper had zero intention of picking up his scythe again, despite being perfectly capable of doing so. It didn't seem fair if he got to keep his powers and I didn't.

"Thanks for nothing, then." My hands curled into fists at my sides, and I walked away from the hut without looking back.

Mart peered over my shoulder. "Want me to deal with him instead?"

"Mart, enough," I hissed. "You don't need him to use his scythe on you."

Especially as I might not be able to get you back this time. That thought sent me down an unpleasant path. It'd been a blatant misuse of my Reaper skills that had enabled me to bind Mart's ghost to the land of the living long after he was supposed to have moved on. Enough that running into the Reaper Council again might well result in them severing our connection, which was reason enough to stay far away from them. He'd been tied to me for more than eight years, and I'd sooner lose my Reaper skills than lose Mart.

But what if those two things were tied together?

The thought sat in my chest like a ball of lead, and my nails dug into my palms as I did my best to shove the thoughts aside. Harold wouldn't dare to bring the Council to Hawkwood Hollow, not when he'd be in real trouble the instant they saw the sheer number of ghosts congregating in town. Besides, he hadn't been speaking from a place of expertise when he'd told me I was losing my Reaper skills. He'd just been as unhelpful as ever.

All the same, a dark cloud hung over my head as I retraced my steps to the inn and found Carey eating breakfast with Casper in the restaurant.

"There you are, Maura." Allie accosted me by the door. "I didn't see you go out."

"I went to ask the Reaper if he'd seen either of the victims' ghosts," I explained, opting out of bringing up my glitching Reaper powers. "He said he wasn't paying attention, which I should have expected."

"I bet." Carey chewed her cereal. "Does he ever pay attention to anything except himself?"

"Nope." I went to grab breakfast from the buffet table, while Mart returned to his new favourite spot in the kitchen near the ovens. A text from Drew hit my phone as

I sat down opposite Carey, but it simply read, *I hope you're okay. Will give an update later.* "Well, that's instructive."

"Huh?" Carey squinted at me across the table. "What's up with you?"

"That Reaper." I put down my phone. "And the pack."

"You said someone else died." Her words faltered. "Yesterday."

"Yeah… a witness to the first werewolf's murder." I rubbed my forehead, my lack of sleep giving me a headache. "Belinda Jennings. The pack got into a scuffle over it, since she's not a shifter and she was wandering in their park. That led to them getting angry at Drew for bringing *me* to help him. It's all fun and games over there."

"They can't blame you for trying to help, surely," she said indignantly.

"No, they can't."

Overhearing, Allie joined us. "I'm sorry if they gave you a hard time, Maura. The pack can be quite… hostile to outsiders. I notice they've stopped coming to the restaurant since all this kicked off."

"So they decided to direct their anger at someone who's been trying to help them." I shook my head. "I'm not invited back there today, so there's no chance of me getting roped into helping with the questioning again, at least."

If anything, we were all better off that way, but my bad mood persisted. I wondered if Drew had managed to get any details of Belinda's presence in the park from witnesses at all, or if the pack had been too fixated on bickering to care that a witch had died on their territory. Most likely the latter, so it looked as if it'd be on Drew and me to bring Belinda's killer to justice. With her ghost absent, the odds on that did not look spectacular.

After Carey left for school, I attempted to boost my mood by downing a couple of espresso shots and taking up residence behind the bar to wait for Jia, but I could barely summon up a smile when she walked in, even though she was wearing a pair of socks patterned with Baby Yoda. "Cute."

"Aren't they?" She wiggled her toes. "You have bags under your eyes the size of flying saucers."

I grunted. "Didn't sleep great last night. Did you hear about Belinda Jennings?"

"What's she done now?"

"Did you not hear she was the witch whose body was found in the werewolves' park?" I'd told Allie over the phone, but I hadn't returned to the inn until after Jia's shift had finished, and she'd gone home by that point.

"No." Her face fell. "Who'd kill poor Belinda? She's harmless."

"I think she saw something she shouldn't have the evening of the first murder," I explained. "She was in the park when I first ran into her. Granted, she didn't seem to be paying much attention to the real world at the time, but we found her body in the same place Davey was killed."

"Oh, no." Her mouth twisted. "Why was she even hanging out in the werewolves' park in the first place?"

"Stargazing, apparently. The pack was up in arms about a witch wandering around their territory, so it got ugly yesterday."

"Did one of them kill her? Not to ask for the morbid details, mind."

"She was poisoned, I think," I answered. "Same as the first victim. Not sure if they killed her in the park or they did it elsewhere and then left her body in the bushes to stop us tracking the killer."

"Why would they do that?" she asked. "Were they trying to frame someone in particular?"

"No clue, but Belinda was harmless enough that she can only have been killed because she witnessed something that night."

"Did you speak to her ghost?"

Here we go again. "Her ghost wasn't around."

Jia blinked at me. "Really? Was that what happened with the other victim?"

"Yeah." I couldn't even blame Belinda's ghost's disappearance on her being a shifter, because she wasn't one. "It's not unheard of for me to be unable to track a spirit. I was going to try summoning a ghost the way a witch or wizard might do it instead, but the coven has been out of fresh ingredients since Mina left, apparently."

"Who told you that?" she asked. "You spoke to the coven recently?"

"Yesterday." Might as well lay it all out in the open. "The apothecary shut down after Angie's death, and when I tried to get into the storeroom, a bunch of Mina's supporters cornered me. After Drew got involved, they told us that they stopped getting deliveries when Mina left town."

"Okay, that's nonsense," she said. "Most herbs are homegrown, and there'd be tantrums left and right if all routine deliveries had stopped altogether."

"So they were lying."

"They don't want you getting into their stores, I bet. They can hold a grudge like you wouldn't believe."

"I believe it," I said. "Half a dozen of them had their wands on me when they caught me. They even booby-trapped the door against intruders."

"That's ridiculous." She scowled. "They don't need to hoard all the town's ingredient supplies. I hardly think they make a habit of summoning ghosts themselves."

Fair point, and another reason they shouldn't have run out of supplies even if they hadn't been getting deliveries. Whether I'd be able to get my hands on them myself without getting into trouble was another matter, though.

"I suppose I can go back and appeal to their consciences." If any of them had one, which was debatable. "Tell them that one of their fellow witches was murdered yesterday. I know she wasn't part of the coven, but still."

"I have an alternative." She shot me a grin. "How would you like to go on a little stealth mission when our shifts are done?"

———

We waited until Carey had returned from school before asking Allie if we could head out for a quick errand.

"Oh, go ahead," Allie said. "I know you're up to something, both of you."

"Three of us," added Mart from behind us. "Don't think I've forgotten my promise."

"Promise?" Jia gave me a questioning look.

"He said that he'd glue himself to me like a shadow to stop me getting into trouble." It probably wasn't wise to try another break-in attempt, but at least I wasn't acting alone this time around.

I still hadn't heard from Drew, except for his brief text to say *good morning* earlier. I tried not to think too hard about it. He had a lot going on, after all, and now the burden of the investigation entirely fell upon his head. I wondered if he'd spoken to the witches himself yet.

Allie waved us off when we left the inn. I doubted she'd be happy if she found out we planned to break into the witches' headquarters again, but she wasn't part of the coven herself, and she knew why I'd gone against the leader the way I had. She'd also paid the price for my actions against Mina Devlin by being unable to find a replacement bartender until Jia had come along, but it wasn't until yesterday that I'd realised the true extent of their lingering faith in their former leader.

"Allie will be calling me a bad influence on you by the week's end," I remarked to Jia as we made our way to the bridge. "Especially as this is my third attempt to get into the witches' headquarters this week."

"You really want to break into the place in broad daylight?" Mart drifted above the water, keeping pace with us.

"Got a better idea?" I strode across the bridge. "With magic, we don't need to wait for the cover of night, besides."

"What did you use to get in last time?" Jia asked me.

"An unseen spell," I said. "I also undid the booby traps on their door, but they must have heard me anyway."

"Can we get into the storeroom without walking through the lobby?"

Without my shadows? Unlikely. "I could try a transportation spell instead, but I've never actually been inside the storeroom before, and it seems a waste of energy when it's only a short distance from the front door. Besides, they'll see the flash of light."

"Then we need them to be distracted."

"I can create a diversion upstairs," Mart offered. "Knock a few things over. They probably don't know I exist, so I can sow some confusion and make sure nobody's downstairs while you two do your thing."

Jia eyed him. "Are you sure?"

A grin spread across his face. "I haven't wreaked any chaos in ages. This will be fun."

"If you say so." I heaved out a breath. "Right, we need to work out the timing. Mart, you'll have a head start. Once you have everyone on the upper floor, come and give us a signal, and we'll run in."

"With unseen charms on, in case anyone comes downstairs," added Jia. "Also, try to make as much noise as possible in case we walk into any booby traps."

"I won't let you down," he promised. "Here we go."

Jia watched him float away. "Hope he's up for this."

"You know, I think he is," I replied. "I underestimated how starved for attention he was. He'd resigned himself to only being able to see and talk to me and the other ghosts. Unless you count Harold the Reaper, and that guy isn't great company."

"He's still around?" She gave a low whistle. "Wow, he must be ancient. Though you Reapers are almost immortal, right?"

"Only official ones." Not me. I'd have an even harder job fitting into human society if I had the ageless quality of a true Reaper, and that was saying a lot.

Maybe that was why I was losing my powers, but I'd barely passed my mid-twenties. I would have expected that I'd be allowed to keep them for a lot longer than that.

Less than a minute later, Mart popped out of nowhere. "Coast's clear."

He vanished again, and we made for the doors to the witches' headquarters. Jia cast a charm-removal spell, while we both made ourselves unseen before entering the lobby. As promised, nobody was around. From upstairs came a series of crashes which sounded like heavy textbooks falling off shelves. Mart's distraction was in full progress, but we'd better hope they all stayed upstairs for the duration.

Moving quickly, I reached the storeroom and cast an unlocking spell on the door. It sprang open, and I walked in, peering at the rows of shelves lined with pungent-smelling bags of herbs and plants, jars of powders, and even oddities like intact animal claws and teeth.

No ingredient deliveries? I never should have fallen for that obvious a ploy. Shaking my head at myself, I began my search for the right ones. Shelf by shelf, I circled the room, taking a mental note of what was there... and what wasn't.

"You have got to be kidding me," I whispered.

"What is it?" Jia asked from outside the door.

"They're gone," I muttered. "The coven's out of every single ingredient for a ghost summoning."

"All of them?" she whispered back. "Let me look."

She moved into the room, while I took her place on lookout duty as she rummaged around behind me. I already knew she wouldn't find them, though. The coven had intentionally removed everything I needed on the off chance that I did succeed in gaining access to the storeroom.

Mart's voice yelled from upstairs. "One-minute warning!"

Time to go. With no other option, we locked the door behind us and made for the exit. I was tempted to ask Mart to torment the witches for a bit longer, but that wouldn't unearth the missing herbs.

I removed the unseen spell when we were out of sight of the witches' headquarters. "I can't believe they did that."

"Did the witches know you wanted to summon a ghost?" she asked. "You told them?"

"I mentioned it yesterday when I tried to convince them to let me into the storeroom by telling them that I was helping Drew with an investigation. I bet they had plenty of supplies at the time."

Who would have taken them? Marie was the obvious choice, but I hadn't the slightest idea whereabouts she'd hidden them. Talk about vindictive.

"True." She muttered a curse under her breath. "What now?"

"Revenge?" Mart floated over to us. "I can haunt them if you like."

"I'd rather we got the ingredients back." There were too many possible places for them to have hidden them, though. They might have picked any cupboard in the coven's headquarters, or in one of their own homes, or even dumped them out in a field somewhere. Who knew?

A buzzing in my pocket alerted my attention. I pulled out my phone, finding Drew was calling me again. *What happened this time?*

10

I answered the phone. "Hey, Drew. Everything okay?"

"Not exactly. Where are you?"

"The high street. What happened? Not another death?"

"No," he replied cryptically. "You're already out, then? Wait, you didn't go back to see the witches?"

"I didn't see them... technically." I glanced over at Jia and Mart. "Turns out they might have been lying about their lack of supplies, but when I got into the storeroom, someone had inconveniently removed all the herbs needed for a ghost-summoning spell."

He swore under his breath. "I'll have someone look into that, but it'll have to wait. Belinda Jennings's body has disappeared from the morgue."

"I'm sorry, what?" Had someone stolen Belinda's body? Why would anyone do such a bizarre thing? "When was this?"

"We're still trying to figure out the details, but it sounds like an intruder broke in. I was going to go talk to them, but it struck me that if there were any witnesses, they might not be living ones."

"I can only sense ghosts, not dead bodies." Wait. "You want me to talk to the local ghosts? If there are any, I mean?"

"It's up to you," he said. "I know you're busy with work..."

And breaking into the coven storeroom, I finished silently. "I can come. It's not a problem. Let me tell my co-worker first, and I can come and meet you."

"I'll be at the police station soon." He ended the call, while Jia gave me a quizzical look.

"Dead bodies?" Mart floated in front of me. "What dead bodies?"

"Someone stole Belinda's body from the morgue."

Jia's brows shot up. "Seriously?"

"Looks that way," I said. "The detective says there's a lack of witnesses, but if a ghost saw the theft—"

"Then we'll find them," Mart interjected.

"You're coming?"

"Obviously. I meant it when I warned you that I'd stick to you like a shadow."

"Good luck," Jia told me. "Should I let Allie know where you are?"

"That'd be great," I said. "I hope it won't take too long, but there's no guarantee."

Mart flew ahead of me. "First murderers and now grave robbers."

"Does it count as grave robbing if the person isn't actually in the ground yet?"

"It's hardly kidnapping, is it?" Mart crossed the road, and I followed, while we argued the semantics of whether it was possible to kidnap someone who was already dead.

Drew showed up in the middle of it, and it was a testament to how he'd grown used to being around me that he didn't react with any surprise to find me arguing with someone he couldn't see.

"Is your brother with you, by any chance?"

"He's decided he's now my shadow, so yes," I answered. "He caused a diversion so that Jia and I could get into the witches' store cupboard. Do they even know Belinda is dead?"

"I assume they do, but to my knowledge, none of them came forward to identify her body," he replied. "If they've been lying about ingredient-supply issues, though, that's grounds for me to order an investigation."

"I think a runaway dead body is more of a cause for concern." I shook my head. "Not that the witches should be off the hook, of course. They're acting like Mina died and her ghost is still running the coven. Maybe they took Belinda's body themselves in another bid to make our lives difficult."

"I highly doubt someone from the coven took her," said Drew. "Mostly because her body was at the morgue in the shifters' part of town. We'll find out pretty quickly if a witch was seen nearby."

Once again, Drew and I made our way through the outskirts of the shifters' park. I did my best to avoid catching anyone's eyes, not keen to listen to more of their disgruntled muttering about Reapers on their territory.

"If not the witches, then who *would* steal a murder victim's body?" I asked Drew. "And why?"

"To provoke the pack into another fight, perhaps," he

suggested. "It took me a long time to calm them down yesterday, and it was only when the chief showed up that they stopped baring their teeth at one another."

I grimaced. "Did they ever stop being more concerned with the fact that a witch was in their park than that she was murdered?"

"I think you can probably guess the answer." When we left the park, he turned a corner down the street and led the way to a squat brick building. "Most of their concerns today revolved around whether the coven would show up to claim the body. Perhaps that's why someone stole it first."

"Does Belinda have family or anything?"

"Not to my knowledge. That said, the funeral would be up to the coven to organise, and if she did turn out to be murdered, the coven leader would need to be informed."

"There isn't one." *You don't say, Maura.* "I'm not sure there's even a substitute. Mina didn't want any potential competition, I guess."

"Exactly." He approached the door to the morgue and went to speak to someone inside.

I made to follow him, but Mart came to a halt at my side. "I think I'll wait out here. Places full of dead people creep me out."

I arched a brow. "They creep *you* out?"

"It's too cold."

"How do you think the bodies feel?" I scanned the area but didn't see any ghosts. "If you spot any ghosts, can you send them my way?"

"I *suppose.*" He spoke in long-suffering tones as if I'd asked him to do some heinous task.

He had a point about the temperature, though. I shivered while Drew and I waited for the shifter who owned the place to come and speak to us, and I didn't see any ghosts inside the building either. Then again, had I really expected any ghosts to hang around the same place as their dead bodies? They tended to haunt places that reminded them of their former lives, not sterile rooms as chilled as the afterworld.

The shifter who owned the place was surprisingly young, his long blond hair tied into a ponytail. "Can I help you?" he asked Drew. "I assume you heard about the theft."

"The body disappeared this morning, is that right?"

"I believe it did," he replied. "I locked the door, same as usual, but someone sneaked in through the back and absconded with the witch's body."

"You didn't see or hear anything?" Drew asked.

"No." The corners of his mouth turned down. "The room in the back is soundproofed to prevent awkwardness in the case of a body turning out not to be dead. It happens more often than you'd think, since werewolf bites can appear to be fatal at first before the victim recovers."

"Vampires too." Hawkwood Hollow didn't have a resident vampire population that I knew of, which was probably for the best given the pack's volatility. "Though in the case of vampires, the victim is bitten, and Belinda wasn't."

"Right," Drew put in. "She was poisoned. Did you confirm the cause of death before her body was stolen?"

The shifter inclined his head. "Informally, anyway, since we weren't able to get an expert on poisons to come in. We couldn't find any of her family to contact, and the coven isn't answering our calls."

Probably because they're going to Mina Devlin's voicemail. Someone really needed to step in and sort the witches out.

"Have you had many visitors today?" asked Drew. "From the pack?"

The shifter was silent for a moment. "Tessa Quinn dropped by to ask if it was true that a witch was killed on our territory."

"Shana's sister." Weird. Had she known Belinda, or had she just been curious to know who the other victim was? "I don't think they're speaking to one another at the moment."

Why would she walk all the way to the morgue when she made a point of avoiding her family, though? Her stealing the body seemed unlikely, although she lived in a remote enough location that she was better equipped than most to dispose of the evidence.

On the other hand, shifters weren't exactly known for being stealthy. How could a werewolf have sneaked into the morgue through the back door without being detected and without forcing the door? On top of the improbability of poisoning two people in public too. A new batch of unanswered questions exploded in the back of my brain, none of which I had an answer for.

Drew took over the questioning while I went on a surreptitious ghost hunt. As expected, no local spirits were anywhere near the morgue itself, while I found Mart reclining on the doorstep.

"Move out of the way," I told him. "I know most people can't see you, but you're supposed to be helping me find any ghostly witnesses."

"There aren't any ghosts." He sprang upright. "Like I told you."

"Then what was the point in coming here?" Irritation rose within me, mostly directed at my misbehaving Reaper powers. "I can't figure out why someone would steal Belinda's body, unless they want everyone to forget she died."

If the witches had even been bothered to begin with, which was debatable.

Drew exited the building to join me. "Nothing?"

I shook my head. "Ghosts… they can get weird about seeing their own corpses. They don't have the same issues with graveyards, but they generally don't come to places like this unless they have a particular reason. Anyway, are you going to speak to Tessa again?"

"She came in before Belinda's body disappeared, so I doubt she saw anything," he replied.

"Jia mentioned seeing Belinda wandering around the field when she first came to town, though," I told him. "I wonder if Shana's sister ever ran into her as well. She did mention weirdos wandering on her property."

"Fair point." His brow crinkled. "I'll freely admit I'm at a loose end when it comes to the missing body, so talking to anyone who won't snap at me about pack politics would be a welcome distraction."

"They're still hassling you, then?" I fell into step with him as we headed north, towards the road leading out of Hawkwood Hollow. "It doesn't sound like they're letting you do your job."

"My job is to ask questions, and I've covered all the major suspects already," he replied. "As for Belinda's murder, it's been utterly impossible to get anyone to come forward with information."

"So who are you going to speak to?" Mart drifted along behind us.

"The sister of the victim's fiancée," I explained. "She lives out in the middle of nowhere and seems to have visited the morgue shortly before the body disappeared."

"Your brother's still here?" asked Drew. "Does he think you're likely to get into trouble?"

"Yes, and I don't trust you to get her out of it," said Mart.

Drew, of course, heard nothing, so I answered instead. "Basically."

"Really." Drew looked over my shoulder. "If *I* can't keep her out of trouble, I'm pretty sure a ghost can't."

"I'm over here!" Mart yelled at him. "He's talking to me as if I'm a piece of furniture."

"You should be glad he's making the effort to include you," I told him. "You're not being nice yourself, besides."

He huffed, sulking the rest of the way through the shifters' part of town. When we reached the country road leading to Tessa's farm, though, he began to take interest in our surroundings again.

His eager eyes scanned the scenery. "I can see for miles!"

"There aren't many ghosts out here. Just so you know." Since it'd rained overnight, the path was much slipperier and muddier than during our last visit, and I began to wish I'd changed out of my work shoes into my boots before leaving the inn. I slipped in a particularly slick patch of mud and caught Drew's arm for balance. "Maybe I should have shadow-walked here instead."

Not that that was an option if my Reaper skills were acting up, but still.

"I think Tessa would have objected if you shadow-walked into her house," Drew remarked. "I'm beginning to understand why she lives all the way out here, away from the pack drama, though."

"It'd help if the pack was willing to cooperate with literally anyone." I let go of his arm and found a less slippery part of the path to walk on. "I can't figure out what the murderer is playing at. I can understand taking out the witness to the first death, but why steal the body? Did they want to make everyone start accusing one another of being body snatchers instead of murderers, or did she hope they'd forget altogether?"

Unfortunately for Belinda, she was just the type of victim everyone *would* overlook. A strange witch who'd never been part of the coven, had no family, and who'd died mysteriously on shifter territory wouldn't stick in their collective memories for long. The coven's own lack of interest didn't help matters either.

We reached Tessa's farmhouse. A growl rippled through the air, and I skidded to a halt in the mud as the huge form of a werewolf sprinted into view, baring her teeth at us.

Mart jumped so violently he did a backflip in midair, while I barely managed to refrain from flinching. "Whoa, Tessa. Chill out."

Drew, who hadn't reacted at all, looked calmly down at her. "It's just us, Tessa."

Tessa shifted into human form with only a fence to hide her nudity, which caused Mart to yelp for an entirely different reason. Unsurprisingly, Tessa didn't notice him, her eyes on Drew and me as she retrieved a rather muddy robe from the bushes to cover herself with. "You should have called."

"I thought you didn't answer the phone," I said.

"Only when I'm not expecting a call. You're back already?"

Despite her initial reaction to our appearance, she didn't seem surprised to see us, which suggested she'd heard the news already. "I'm guessing you know the latest?"

"That Belinda Jennings was murdered and then someone stole her body? Yes, I do."

"We went to the morgue earlier, and they told me that you visited before the body disappeared," Drew said. "Any particular reason?"

"I only heard of Belinda's death this morning, so I went to the morgue to check if it was the person I thought it was," she said. "I didn't know her name."

"But you did know her?" I asked. "Is she one of the weirdos who trespassed on your property, by any chance?"

"She hasn't done that for a while, but she had a habit of wandering around the fields."

"You didn't attack her, did you?"

"There were a couple of close calls." She shrugged. "She's harmless, though. She just drifted around looking up at the sky through those weird binoculars of hers."

"The ones she couldn't actually see through," I added. "Did she tell you she was a Seer?"

"Might have mentioned it." A breeze hit us from behind, almost carrying Tessa's robe away with it.

Drew, to his credit, kept his eyes on her face. "May we come in?"

Tessa made for the farmhouse and nudged open the door. "Sure."

"No way," Mart said. "Absolutely not. She nearly killed me."

"You're already dead," I muttered, and Tessa gave me an odd look. I'd rather not have to explain the details of my brother's ghost tailing me everywhere, so I left him outside and followed Tessa and Drew into the farmhouse.

Tessa lounged on the rug in front of the fire again. "If you want to know who I think was responsible for the witch's death, I have no idea. Or why, either."

"She made a couple of weird comments around the time Davey's body was found," I commented. "I thought she might have seen something at the park, and I guess the killer must have assumed the same."

She grunted. "I take it nobody has come forward with information?"

"Not even to claim the body," Drew said. "Have you seen her at all since Davey's death?"

"Once." She wrinkled her forehead. "Or twice, perhaps. She didn't come near the house, but I saw her wandering around the field, carrying a sack over her shoulder."

"A sack of what?" I asked. "How big?"

She measured a small distance between her hands. "Maybe this big? I didn't see what she did with it, and she never noticed I was watching her."

Strange, but given Belinda's previous behaviour, it might not be worth assigning too much meaning to the weird things she'd done.

"Have you spoken to your sister in the last couple of days?" I asked.

"Definitely not." A touch of defensiveness entered her tone. "She's too stubborn to apologise to me for what she said during our argument."

"Why not try?" I ventured. "She must be really upset about Davey, whatever her motives in marrying him."

"Maura has a point," said Drew. "From what I observed, the chief seems largely disinterested in comforting his daughter. He's mostly been trying to divert blame from his family—your family, that is."

She blinked. "Who blamed our family?"

"Nobody that I know of," Drew answered. "That said, Davey's own friends are irked that the chief and his companions seem to be spreading rumours that someone in their own faction of the pack was responsible for murdering him."

"You mean someone who isn't a fan of the chief." She gave him an assessing look. "That covers a fair few people, but I'd have to wonder why they'd kill the groom and not the bride. She's the chief's potential successor, after all. Not Davey."

Yeah. That's weird. No weirder than the fact that a witch with seemingly no connection to either had been the next victim, though.

"Do you think Shana will try to marry again?" I asked. "From what I heard, she wants out of that house. Davey's own brother knew she didn't care for Davey in the same way he cared for her."

Her brow arched. "Did he?"

"Yes, he did," said Drew. "Is there a reason she saw marriage as her only way out?"

"She's lazy," Tessa replied. "And she assumes she'll be the next chief by default and that the position will fall on her head without any effort."

"What about the fine-arts degree?" I asked. "I imagine she can easily afford the fees, but she must have at least passed some exams to get into university."

"Sure, she's smart enough, I guess," Tessa acknowledged. "No practical skills, though. She was glad I got the farm and not her. It used to be our grandparents'."

Maybe, but Shana had remained trapped with her controlling, judgmental parents all the same. Her family had no reason to have murdered her husband-to-be, but then again, why would the chief be so eager to divert blame from himself that he'd intentionally anger another segment of the pack by spreading baseless rumours?

In any case, Tessa plainly had no idea who'd killed Belinda, let alone taken her body, so Drew brought an end to the questioning.

I left the farmhouse first and found Mart drifting around the field. "It's so empty out here. I miss the ghosts."

"I wouldn't go that far." I sidestepped another muddy puddle. "If Tessa gets as many weirdo visitors as she claims, she might have to invest in security which doesn't involve shifting and scaring away anyone who comes near her house."

"Weirdos." Mart scoffed. "I'm not the one walking naked in the rain."

"It's not raining at the moment." A droplet fell on my face, as if to disprove my point. "All right, we'd better get back to town."

"Agreed." Drew took the lead, while I cursed my nonpractical work shoes as I followed him. Mart wolf-whistled at me when Drew caught my hand, but I'd happily endure his commentary if it meant I didn't fall flat on my face in the mud. Besides, I liked it when Drew held my hand. It didn't hurt that Tessa's… well, *assets,* hadn't distracted him either. Being surrounded by shifters probably made one unbothered by casual nudity.

In any case, our visit to Tessa had proven that Belinda had been roaming the fields recently but not that anyone else had been watching her. No, the person who'd killed her had struck on shifter territory. Regardless, they must know Drew wouldn't easily drop the investigation, so that couldn't be why they'd taken her body. And what of Davey's?

I asked Drew as much. "Did the morgue release Davey's body?"

"They did, and the family had a private burial ceremony this morning. I briefly checked in with them, but it wasn't long after that that the morgue called me."

"Watch that the grave robbers don't dig up Davey too," warned Mart.

I glanced at him. "There'd be no logical reason in stealing the bodies of either victim, surely."

"No," said Drew. "That said, it's still the murderer who concerns us the most."

"Except Belinda's body is still missing, and nobody seems to care but us." Including the witches. "Want to talk to Marie and the rest of the coven to see if they're hiding any more nefarious secrets?"

"Not particularly," Drew replied. "I rather think I'm overdue for another visit to the chief."

11

It was with apprehension that I accompanied Drew back to the werewolves' area of town. The rain eased off while we walked, but despite the sun peeking at us from behind the clouds, the gloomy atmosphere persisted.

"Are you sure the chief wants to see me?" He hadn't been as outright rude as his daughter had, but he definitely hadn't treated me with any level of respect either. "I think it's safe to say I'm unlikely to find any ghosts at this point."

"Perhaps not, but you often think of questions I don't," Drew told me. "Like with Tessa."

"Her sister pretty much told me to get lost, though." I came to a sudden halt when I recognised two werewolves on the opposite side of the street: Lewis Rogers and Ian, the guy who worked at the newsagent.

"Ian." Drew recognised him, too, veering in their direction.

Lewis looked us over, his mouth pulling down at the

corners, while Ian simply gave the detective a nod and kept walking.

"If you're going to see the chief, I'd appreciate it if you told him to stop hassling my parents," Lewis growled under his breath. "They've had to go away for a week or so to get away from him."

"Seriously?" I blinked. "They left town?"

"Is that so strange?" he said defensively. "They've had a ghastly week already."

He caught up with Ian and left us behind, while Drew and I exchanged glances. *That's weird.* Or not, given the rising tension following Davey's death and the pack's arguments on top of that. "Drew, did anyone tell you that Davey's parents left?"

"No," he replied. "It's lucky that I didn't need to question them again, though I do have questions about the timing."

"What, you think they ran off with Belinda's body?" I didn't think they'd even met her, alive or dead.

"No, but there's something odd about the situation." He continued onward through shifter territory. "I'll have to ask Lewis some more questions later. I'm surprised to see him walking around in the open."

"He can't hide away forever, though." Maybe that meant the open accusations had died down, but I somehow doubted that was the case.

All the same, his parents' disappearance lingered in the back of my mind while we approached the chief's home. Drew led the way through the front gate, while Mart drifted behind us and looked admiringly at the house. "Ooh, fancy."

"Isn't it?" I followed Drew. "Don't make too much noise in there. The chief can't see you, but he can see *me*."

Shana must have been watching our approach from the window because she answered the door scarcely a moment after Drew rang the doorbell. "Back again?"

"Yes, we are," said Drew. "You heard—"

"Yes, I heard that someone swiped the witch's body from the morgue," she interrupted. "My dad said it was probably the coven."

"Belinda wasn't part of the coven," I told her. "Also, there isn't one anymore, technically."

"Detective." Mrs Quinn walked into the hall behind her daughter. "And... Mary."

"Maura," I corrected. "May we come in and talk to the chief?"

"He's a busy man."

Shana scoffed. "He's got his feet up, watching football at the moment. He can spare a few minutes."

Mrs Quinn gave her a thin-lipped look. "I'll tell him. You can wait in the lobby, Detective."

"Isn't she nice?" Mart said. "Both of them, even."

"Quiet," I whispered to him. "If the chief's in a bad mood, then I don't need to make it worse by conversing with ghosts."

Not getting the hint, he flew into the house behind us, making approving noises at the fancy decor.

Meanwhile, Drew waylaid Shana before she could follow her mother. "If you don't mind, I have a couple of questions I'd like to ask you alone."

"Alone?" she echoed. "You already asked me enough questions at the park yesterday. I didn't know the witch who died. And I don't see why you felt the need to bring your girlfriend into our house again. She's not a detective; she's a ghost hunter."

"Maybe you've got ghosts in your house." Mart mimicked rabbit ears behind her head with his fingers. "There's one haunting you right this instant."

Drew glanced at me. "I told you, Maura's helping me with the investigation."

"She's hardly even a ghost hunter," Shana continued. "She couldn't even *find* the witch's ghost yesterday."

Okay, that was uncalled for. "What *is* your problem with me? You were all set to marry a relative stranger to get out of your parents' house, and you think me dating Drew is more of an issue?"

"How dare you judge me?" She whipped around and stalked across the entrance hall. "You haven't lived here under the chief's eye, listening to his constant criticism, knowing you'll never be taken seriously. You haven't a clue what it's like to be me."

"I know you're a brat," Mart called after her.

I was tempted to say the same myself, but I managed to refrain. "Your sister lived here, too, and she didn't need to marry a stranger to escape." Her penchant for nudity and her habit of attacking trespassers aside, I actually quite liked Tessa.

"You talked to *her?*" Shana turned on her heel, eyes narrowing. "I never should have planted the idea in your head."

"I always planned to talk to all the potential culprits for Belinda Jennings's murder," Drew interjected. "And I'd appreciate it if you didn't try to pick a fight with Maura. She's been a great help."

"Your sister visited the morgue yesterday," I added. "Did you know?"

"What?" Shana said blankly. "You think she's the one who stole the witch's body? Is that what you're saying?"

"No, I'm not," I replied. "I can tell you're as stubborn as she is, but you might want to listen to her advice occasionally. You don't have to do what the chief says."

"He's the most powerful person in the pack, so I'd say I do." Her mouth clamped shut when her mother walked back in.

"He'll see you in five minutes." Mrs Quinn addressed Drew, outright ignoring me. "Shana, are you okay? I heard you shouting."

"I'm perfectly fine," Shana growled through gritted teeth. "They've been hassling Tessa."

"Oh." Mrs Quinn's gaze dropped, her cheeks reddening a little. "Did Tessa say anything? About, ah, the deaths?"

"Don't you talk to her?" I asked, surprised.

"She left the pack, and my husband is not a forgiving man."

That figured. The entire family was too stubborn for their own good. "Did you know he's been spreading rumours accusing Davey's friends of murder?"

Her mouth fell open, and Shana winced. In the background, Mart howled with laughter. "Good one."

Mrs Quinn turned on Drew. "Are you going to let her bad-mouth your chief in his own house?"

"Maura simply spoke the truth," said Drew. "I've heard from numerous sources that your husband has been fuelling the rumours himself."

"Have *you* been outside and heard the rumours?" I asked her.

"No." She sounded affronted. "I've been lying low since your investigation brought every feud in the entire pack to the surface."

"You mean the murders," I corrected. "That's what got everyone mad. Our investigation wouldn't be necessary if someone hadn't died."

Shana laughed. "You think it's necessary?"

"Excuse me? Your fiancé is dead."

"And you've done a stellar job of finding the culprit so far," Shana bit out.

"That's enough," warned Drew. "If you'd prefer not to find the killer, then that's your prerogative."

"Of course I want to find the killer." Her eyes sparkled with sudden angry tears. "Stop twisting my words."

"You just said you think the investigation is a waste of time." If she expected me to be sympathetic, she might have tried holding back the insults towards Drew and me. Her mother, meanwhile, hovered in the background, wringing her hands helplessly. If anything, that annoyed me more than her daughter's belligerence.

"Have you really never left home in the past few days?" asked Drew. "I thought you studied at university."

She shrugged. "I can afford to skip a few lectures. Better than being ambushed with pity at every corner."

"Why did you decide to study fine arts?" Her attitude aside, her choice of study seemed to be a point of contention with her parents and her sister.

"Why are *you* suddenly so interested?" she retaliated. "Has my sister been telling everyone what a failure I am?"

"No, she simply answered my questions," Drew told

her. "All she wanted was for you to make up your mind about your future."

"I made up my mind, and then someone *murdered* my fiancé." Her hands clenched. "She likes that rotten old farmhouse of hers, but I can't stand that kind of life. I'd go mad."

"You live in a nice house." To say the least. "You're not hurting for cash either, I bet."

Her face flushed. "You're good at poking your nose in where it doesn't belong, aren't you?"

"Shana," said her mother, but there was no heat in her words. "Please try to be polite. The detective is trying to find Davey's killer, despite his... irrelevant questions."

"They aren't irrelevant." I looked between them. "Who's to say she can't get a job with an arts degree? Is that what the chief told her?"

Mrs Quinn gave a nervous glance behind her. "We've always been supportive of her choices. She *is* the chief's heir to the pack leadership, though."

"I think you and I both know that position isn't hereditary." Drew addressed Mrs Quinn. "The pack was once run in that way, yes, but that is no longer the case."

Shana made a sceptical noise. "For some people, it is. Dad's rivals would love to get their hands on our title."

And you decided to solve that problem by marrying one of them? I managed to hold back that comment... barely. "Were you aware that Davey's parents seem to have left town?"

Her eyes widened a fraction. "Did they?"

"Yes," said Drew. "I assumed you knew. Didn't you see them at the burial?"

"What?" she spluttered. "What burial?"

I gave Drew an alarmed look. "Er, maybe they wanted to keep it to the family only."

The chief had known, surely... right?

Shana's face went bright red. "They didn't tell *me* that."

"Shana..." Her mother flinched when Shana turned on her.

"You knew, didn't you?" Her eyes glimmered with tears. "I don't believe this. You want me to forget about him, don't you?"

"No, of course not, but your father said—"

Shana stormed off, leaving her mother midsentence, and disappeared up a winding staircase to the upper floor. I heard her thumping about upstairs and had to admit that I had trouble imagining her being stealthy enough to sneak into the morgue and steal a body.

Mrs Quinn watched her daughter leave, but she didn't follow her. "She's easily upset these days."

"I thought she knew," Drew said apologetically. "You didn't let her attend the burial of her own husband-to-be?"

"The chief wanted to keep her out of the public eye."

"How is she coping?" Drew asked. "She seems very upset."

Keep her out of the public eye? Hadn't she been in the park yesterday when we'd found Belinda's body? The chief was definitely bending the truth when it suited him, but it was beyond me to figure out if that pointed towards guilt or not.

"She's very high-strung," said Mrs Quinn. "She *is* twenty. I got married at her age, but I do wonder if she should wait a few more years."

"If she did, would she live with you in the meantime?"

I asked. "Because I think she wants a place of her own. Not like the farmhouse either."

The farmhouse wasn't fancy at all, suggesting that it must have belonged to the non-chief side of their family. It also made me wonder if Mrs Quinn hadn't married Chief Quinn for a similar reason.

Mrs Quinn cleared her throat, looking uncomfortable. "There aren't many jobs available to new graduates in her discipline."

"You're loaded." No point in underplaying it. "She gets an allowance, doesn't she?"

"That isn't…" She broke off with a glance behind her. "Oh, my husband is ready to see you."

In the living room, Drew and I found Chief Quinn sitting in the same armchair as before. He wore a disinterested look on his face. "I hope this is important."

"If you were aware, Belinda Jennings's body was stolen from the morgue earlier today," Drew began.

"Yes, I was aware." An impatient note underlaid his voice. "I'm also busy. So if you don't mind getting to the point, I'd appreciate it."

"Did you know Davey Rogers's parents have left town?" Drew went on.

"No," said Chief Quinn. "Did they leave after the burial?"

"It's my understanding that they've had to deal with a fair bit of harassment," replied Drew. "From your section of the pack."

"Did they now?" Anger painted red splotches on his cheeks. "I thought you considered yourself part of the pack, Detective."

"I do, but I wouldn't be doing my job if I didn't ask you

about the details," Drew told him. "The fact remains that your name has come up several times in connection with these rumours, and while your daughter claims to have been kept at home, she was at the park yesterday, as you saw yourself."

"What do you want me to say?" He rose to his feet. "I can't control everything she does. She's a grown woman."

You don't treat her like that most of the time. "You didn't tell her about Davey's burial."

"That was the responsibility of the one who organised it," he growled. "His family has decided to act as though we were never tied to begin with. It's an insult."

If he'd accused Davey's friends of murdering him, then frankly, it wasn't a surprise that Davey's family hadn't wanted anything to do with the chief.

Drew's mouth pressed together. "They suffered a horrific tragedy. Did you make an effort to get in touch with them after Davey's death? To my knowledge, they haven't spoken to you in person since beforehand."

Seriously? He'd hardly been acting like a benevolent leader who cared about his people, that was for sure.

"They refused my invitation to meet with me, and I was too busy to seek them out myself."

"That's strange," said Drew. "I'm sure you've been near their part of town recently. Lewis Rogers saw you himself, in fact."

"Did he now?" A dangerous glint appeared in his eye. "Are you accusing me of lying?"

Oh, boy. The last thing we needed was to start a fight with the chief, but it couldn't be more obvious that he'd lied openly to the head of the police force and more besides.

Drew paused for a fraction of a second. "I think this discussion is going to be unproductive, Chief. However, I'd like to talk to your daughter again."

I was all too happy to get out of there. I managed to hold my tongue until we reached the lobby again, at which point I lowered my voice. "Does being chief mean he can get away with blatantly lying?"

"No," Drew murmured back. "If I accuse him openly, though, we won't be able to talk to Shana again."

"Why do you want to?" She wasn't in a great mood herself, though she'd been a fraction more honest than both her parents.

Mart flew downward to meet us. "Has he stopped yelling yet?"

"I wondered where you'd gone."

"I wanted to look around. This house is amazing."

True, but were the family not as well-off as they appeared? Or was I reading too much into their apparent lack of faith in Shana to earn a living for herself? I didn't see how they could have a fancy house like this and not have tons of cash stockpiled, but now that I thought on the subject, the position of pack chief wasn't typically well paid and was supposed to be more of a voluntary thing. I'd need to ask Drew for the details.

Drew himself made for the stairs. "I want to see if we can coax a few more answers out of Shana."

"Did the chief buy this house with the money he earned from leading the pack?"

"No, Chief Quinn inherited it from his parents."

"So he might be broke."

"If he is, he's hidden it from everyone else for a long while."

The same thought had occurred to Drew, then. Yet Shana must still have more money than Davey based on the house alone. So many details still didn't add up, and while I didn't hold out much hope of gaining Shana's cooperation, I was out of any better ideas.

Shana's room was easy to find, with a bronze plaque carrying her name on the door, reminiscent of Mina Devlin's office. Drew knocked on the door. "Shana?"

She didn't answer, but from the way the door moved inward, it wasn't locked. Another knock brought no response.

"I don't think she's in." I pushed open the door anyway. "Oh, wow."

Paintings covered every surface in the wide bedroom. *Good* ones, as far as I could tell with my lack of knowledge of what constituted skill at artwork. She must have spent hours working on each one. An easel stood against the back wall.

Drew entered the room behind me, looking around at the artwork.

"Check that out." I gestured to the collection of paintings. "I think she was selling herself short."

"I'm inclined to agree."

What had Davey thought of her passion? I should have asked Shana earlier, but she hadn't given the impression that she'd been hiding a treasure trove like this in her room. Unable to help myself, I walked farther in to get a better look at the painting pinned to the easel, and then something caught my eye on the table which made my heart swoop downward.

Lying on a nearby table were Belinda Jennings's binoculars. "How'd these get here? Did they disappear at the same time as her body?"

"Yes." His eyes shadowed. "This is going to cause trouble."

"No kidding." Hadn't the chief insisted that Shana had never left the property in the past few days? Aside from her excursion to the park… and everything else he'd lied about. I picked up the binoculars and left the room, heading for the stairs.

Where Shana had disappeared to was frankly the least of our problems. Had she stolen Belinda's body as an act of defiance? What would be the point, though? And why bring the binoculars in here?

We found Mrs Quinn pacing the lobby, her hands twisting together. "Shana went outside. What have you got there?"

Drew took the binoculars from me and held them up. "We found these in your daughter's room."

"Excuse me?" She stopped midstep. "What are those?"

"They belonged to Belinda Jennings, the witch who was murdered," I answered.

All the colour drained from her face. "No. This is a mistake. A misunderstanding."

"I hope it is," said Drew. "Having seen what your daughter created in her room, it's clear she's very talented."

Mrs Quinn swayed on the spot. "That can't be possible. Someone planted them there."

"Someone broke into your house and planted the property of someone who was murdered in your daughter's room?" Drew queried.

Her own parents, maybe? That made little sense, especially for the chief, but anyone else would have had a hard time breaking in without being caught, surely. Unless the chief had no security aside from the high fences, which weren't necessarily a deterrent to a determined werewolf. I hadn't seen any household staff either.

Drew made for the back door, as did I. "You don't think Belinda's body is hidden here too?" I asked him.

"At this point, we have to expect the unexpected."

Outside, Shana paced in circles on the paved yard at the front of the expansive garden, and from the angry look on her face, she hadn't calmed down in the slightest. "What are you doing out here?"

"I am conducting a search of the property," Drew told her. "Given what we found in your room."

"You were in my *room?*" Outrage flitted across her face. "Did you touch anything up there?"

"Those." I indicated the binoculars. "We found them in your room."

An angry flush lit up her features. "You put them there yourselves, didn't you?"

"Believe me, we didn't." I scanned the garden, but the neat lawns and paving stones didn't show any signs that someone had dug a hole to bury a body. "These binoculars vanished from the morgue along with their owner."

Was it an act of revenge from Davey's part of the pack? Or was the murderer trying to stir up discord to cover up their own crimes? Either was possible, but framing the chief's daughter was asking for trouble.

"Get out," Shana snapped. "You're not content with meddling in my love life, but you want to have me arrested, don't you? Someone is trying to frame us."

"The person who planted those binoculars in your

room is the one who wanted you arrested," I told her. "Do you have any idea who that might be?"

I was giving her the benefit of the doubt, considering she was equally likely to have stolen them herself, but her face reddened even further at my comment. "I don't have to answer to the likes of you."

"Shana," said Drew warningly.

"Or you." She wheeled around to face him. "You're out of the pack. My dad will see to it."

"Shana." Her mother's tremulous voice came from behind us. "Calm down."

"He accused Dad of lying," she spat. "He's trying to get us arrested. That Reaper Witch corrupted him."

I abandoned all notions of civility. "You're broke, aren't you? That's the big secret."

Shana's jaw gaped open in horror. Mrs Quinn flushed even brighter red. And Drew cleared his throat. "I will return to talk to you later with the full backup of my team, and I expect you to be ready to share all the details with me."

My instincts protested against leaving, but getting trapped in the pack chief's back yard when my Reaper skills were acting up did not strike me as a good idea. So I followed Drew to the exit, clenching my shaking hands at my sides.

"Sorry," I whispered to him. "I shouldn't have provoked them."

"You said what needed to be said, Maura," he murmured. "I can't believe I never noticed the chief's financial situation before."

"Does it link to the murder, though?" I asked. "Because if they wanted Shana to marry for money, killing the guy doesn't make much sense."

He shook his head. "No, it doesn't."

"Neither does stealing those." I reached for the binoculars.

"Maybe she stole them to sell," Mart supplied, having drifted over to join us again on our way out.

"Are they worth anything, though?" They looked like regular binoculars to me. I held them up to my eyes, but as I'd suspected, I couldn't see past the painted fabric.

"Keep those," said Mart. "They suit you."

"Very funny." I lowered my hands. "Drew, are you sure it's a wise idea to talk to them alone? Because I wouldn't put it past the chief to shift and attack you if you came out and accused him openly."

"Precisely why I need the full support of my department to search his house," he said. "Don't worry about me, Maura. I've arrested shifters before when they've been in wolf form and survived."

"That doesn't sound very reassuring, Drew." I didn't need him to get a limb ripped off, thanks. "Besides, I'm not sure you'll find Belinda's body in their house."

As to why they'd kill poor Davey when he was less well off than they were… that remained to be seen.

12

By the time we reached the police station, I'd given myself a headache, trying to make sense of the recent bombshells which had landed on our heads. I let Drew go into the station to update his colleagues and waited outside.

"I know I shouldn't go back," I said to myself—or rather, to Mart. "But I don't want Drew to face that awful family alone."

"They're equally mad at you," he reminded me. "Not that Shana didn't deserve what you said to her."

"She's obnoxious." Then again, the rest of her family was just as bad, with the exception of Tessa. "And she was lying openly. Her dad too. They started the rumours and tried to feign innocence even after they drove Davey's parents out of town. Chief Quinn was lying to Drew's face too. He can't possibly keep being chief after this."

"First you disrupt the coven and now the werewolf pack." Mart snickered. "Are you going to depose the Reaper Council next?"

"No." Honestly. It was no wonder the ghosts had thrived in Hawkwood Hollow while nobody else had. "And he's not been deposed yet. I don't see him stepping down easily."

Movement caught my eye on the other side of the road, and I recognised Ian, walking back to his shop with his hands in his pockets.

Before I could quite think through my decision, I crossed the road to meet him. "Hey."

"Oh, it's you." He did not sound particularly enthusiastic. "I went for a walk—"

"With Lewis Rogers," I finished. "I saw, remember? Did you know his parents had left town?"

"He told me himself," said Ian. "Shame, really, but I don't blame them."

"Not with the chief spreading rumours that one of his friends had him killed."

He winced. "I hope Lewis has the sense to keep his mouth shut in front of anyone who knows the chief."

"Drew's going to take a team to the chief's house to confront him over it, so none of you will have to worry about him for long."

He paled. "I wouldn't do that if I valued my safety."

"Drew has the law on his side," I reminded him. "Chief Quinn lied for the purposes of stirring up conflict. That isn't exactly pack-leader behaviour, is it?"

"He was only trying to do what he thought was best for the pack. He didn't know…"

"Didn't know what?" I pressed. "If Davey's parents had to leave town over the rumours he spread, then that doesn't paint him in a positive light. Unless you know something else? About Belinda's death and her body's disappearance?"

"No," he said. "I don't know the witch. I was sorry she died and even sorrier that she became a pawn in the pack's games."

True, perhaps, but I was positive that he'd been meaning to say something else entirely. "What were you and Lewis discussing, aside from his parents leaving town?"

"Nothing much."

"You can tell me anything, and I won't tell the chief," I reassured him. "I don't want Drew to get on the chief's bad side if it's unnecessary, but we found evidence that his daughter took something of the second victim's which went missing from the morgue along with her body, so he's obligated to search their house regardless of whether he spread the rumours himself or not."

He sucked in a breath. "Not a wise idea. He can apply the law if he likes, but it won't do any good."

"Says who?" When he motioned towards his shop, I walked behind him. "Look, I don't even have to tell Drew if you really don't want me to, but two people are dead and another two left town directly because of the chief's actions. If you know anything—"

"Ask her," he blurted. "Ask her sister."

"Whose, Shana's?"

He closed the door behind him in answer. I might have followed, but Mart shoved his hand through me from behind, bringing an uncomfortable rush of cold to my spine. "The detective is back."

I spun around. Sure enough, Drew was crossing the

road to join me. When he reached my side of the pavement, his gaze went to the newsagent. "Were you talking to Ian?"

"Yeah, he seemed pretty freaked out about something." I lowered my voice. "He said not to provoke the chief and to ask Tessa for the details if I want to know why. Whatever *that* means."

"Tessa?" He frowned. "The rest of the department are tied up in meetings, so I can speak to her again while I wait for them to be ready to see the chief. What details did he tell us to ask her about, though?"

"I have no idea." I glanced at Ian's shop. "He insisted the chief was trying to protect the pack, which I doubt, but he also implied Tessa knows something more. Besides, she might have seen Davey's parents leaving town if they headed north."

"Fair point."

For the second time that day, we began our journey out of Hawkwood Hollow. Mart flew behind us, while I did my best to ignore the sinking suspicion that even Tessa might be culpable in her family's crimes, however heinous they might be.

It didn't help that more shifters were out on the streets than before. Stares followed Drew and me, whispers passing between the shifters as though I was a slug someone had trodden into the carpet.

"Have they forgotten they're mad at each other?" I asked. "Or are they like Shana, and they think it's all my fault for getting my human-Reaper hands all over the case?"

"Ignore them, Maura," he said. "I'm glad I have you with me."

Despite the warmth conjured up by his words, I couldn't deny that my involvement in the case had been a massive failure so far, and the knock-on effect on Drew's reputation only made the wound sting worse. This was a prime example of why I'd avoided involving myself in paranormal communities in the past. Things had a tendency to spiral out of control around me, and if I brought the pack into the same level of drama as I had the local coven, then I could only imagine how much trouble Drew would have on his hands.

It came as a great relief when we reached the country road out of town, although the path was even muddier than it'd been earlier.

"Do you think Tessa was secretly helping her family cover up Davey's death?" I asked Drew. "Because I'll be pretty sad if the one Quinn I liked turns out to be a murderer."

"She has an alibi. She's also self-sufficient and would have no need to marry for money like Shana did."

"Still not quite getting that part, to be honest," I admitted. "Look at their house. Couldn't they just sell a few antiques if they needed some quick cash?"

"I don't know all the details yet."

"I can understand why Shana picked her university course now, anyway." I trod around a slippery patch of mud to avoid losing my balance. "I guess shifters don't have a great admiration for the arts."

"Not generally," he replied. "They think practical skills have more value."

"Honestly, a lot of humans think the same. Pity, because she's really good."

Too bad she might end up in a prison cell unless she

gave Drew a very good reason for having those binoculars in her room. Belinda's body, though, had been nowhere to be found. The image of someone carrying a bag into the field appeared in my mind's eye, and I nearly slipped onto my back.

"Whoa." Drew reached out an arm to steady me. "You okay?"

I caught my balance. "Yeah, but I'm reminded of why I'm not a fan of hiking."

My thoughts remained on Tessa's earlier comment. Had she unconsciously given herself away when she'd mentioned Belinda carrying a bag outside of the town? It was a stretch, I'd admit, but the fields and muddy trenches certainly contained ample space to bury a body if one was so inclined, and it was entirely possible that Shana had sneaked the body out of town and left Tessa to do the rest of the work.

As I slipped again, Drew held my arm to keep me from falling over. "It's easier to move in wolf form out here."

Mart glided alongside us, his arms spread out as if to catch the wind. "Maura wouldn't object if you shifted and lost your clothes."

I ignored my brother. "Am I being ridiculous when I ask if there's a chance Belinda's body might have been buried out here?"

"No," said Drew. "I had the same thought myself."

To my great relief, Tessa didn't ambush us in wolf form this time around. When we reached the farmhouse, she walked out on foot, properly dressed for once and even wearing shoes. "What in the world are you doing out here again?"

"We found Belinda Jennings's binoculars in your parents' house," Drew explained.

Shock rippled across her face. "You found what?"

"Shana told us that they were planted in her room," I told her. "So did your parents."

She swore under her breath. "Who would do that?"

"I don't know, but listen, you have to tell us what you know." I spoke faster, aware of Drew's presence at my side. "Ian was adamant that we shouldn't accuse the chief of anything, even though we know for a fact he's been spreading rumours about the murderer being one of Davey's companions. Davey's parents have since left town. Did you see them on their way out?"

Tessa gave me a rueful look. "Is it that obvious?"

"No, but if you have anything to tell us, it might prevent me from getting into a fight with the chief," said Drew. "Maura, for one, would be relieved if I didn't have to risk my neck."

Her shoulders slumped. "I don't know if this is going to help, but Davey... he had a stroke of luck the day he died. Turns out he won a fortune on a lottery ticket."

My mouth fell open. "What?"

Whatever I'd expected her to say, it wasn't that.

"Yeah, his parents told me," she went on. "They took the money with them when they left. Obviously, they didn't want the chief to get hold of it. With their son being dead, it wasn't like they were obligated to give him any of it anyway, but the chief might have got them tied up in pack politics and found a way to wrangle some of the cash."

"Did the chief know?" If he had, it was an obvious

reason for him to murder Davey, but not Belinda. As for the missing body? That was still a mystery.

"I haven't spoken to him, so I don't know," she said. "But it's obvious why Davey's parents were in a hurry to leave town."

Because they had money, which would help a broke and incompetent werewolf chief trying to hide his own lack of funds. Question was, how would we get from there to proof of Davey's murder? And how could Drew arrest the chief without provoking a fight with his entire faction of the pack?

"What about Belinda?" Drew asked. "Her body vanished. You already told me you don't know where she is."

"I don't," she said. "In fact, I didn't know about any of this until Davey's parents left town early this morning. When I came out to talk to them, they told me that they were going away for a while."

"Where to, do you know?" I asked.

She shook her head. "I honestly have no idea, but I'm sorry I didn't tell you earlier, Detective."

"It's the rest of your family who are of more concern to me at the moment," he said. "Your sister had an item belonging to a murder victim in her room. I assume Davey's parents putting it there is out of question, but would she have taken it herself?"

She shook her head violently. "No way. She wouldn't have."

"Would anyone have wanted to set her up?" I asked.

Tessa's mouth pressed together. "I'll talk to her. Maybe she'll be willing to have a discussion with me if she has to choose between resuming contact or getting arrested."

"I certainly hope so," said Drew. "The pack seems to think I'm out to make trouble, not to solve the murders."

Yeah, but they wouldn't think that if I hadn't come here with you. The words flitted through my mind, unwanted but undeniable.

Mart zipped over to us. "I don't see any dead bodies, but I can't dig under the ground."

I looked past him at the fields, where the sun had begun to descend upon the horizon. "Before we leave, I think we should have a look around for anything buried out here."

"What, did you think I buried Belinda's body?" Tessa snorted. "I suppose a field *is* a logical place to dispose of a body, but I definitely haven't seen anyone walking around with a shovel."

Unless Davey's parents had stolen Belinda's body, but that made no sense either.

"You mentioned seeing her wandering around with a bag. Whereabouts?"

She pointed across the field towards a muddy ditch on the other side of the fence dividing it from the neighbouring field. "There."

I walked in that direction, Mart flying ahead of me. Drew caught me up at the edge of the muddy trench, his gaze roving around. Looking for footprints, maybe. Having werewolf senses would come in handy, but I was stuck with two feet and a limited range of vision. I didn't see any footprints, human or otherwise, but the rain-slick mud made it difficult to tell.

When I slipped over and fell on my rear, Mart laughed at me so hard that he flipped upside down. I kicked mud in his general direction when I was back on my feet.

"You'll ruin my shoes!" he protested.

"Look at the state of mine." I took one step and immediately slid over again. Mart howled with laughter, while I lunged at him. My foot caught on something solid that sent me flying into a patch of bushes.

"Ha!" Mart circled me from above. "That was priceless. I wish I could store that image in my mind forever."

"Ow." I crawled to my feet. "Stop laughing at me and help me look for whatever tripped me up."

"Did you trip over a dead body?" he snickered. "Actually, that's exactly the kind of thing you'd do."

Mourning my muddy clothes and my dignity, I scanned the mud for the offending obstacle.

"Maura?" Drew called to me. "Are you okay?"

I gave him a thumbs-up with my mud-covered hands.

"Found it!" Mart pointed. "Look, there *is* a hole in the ground."

I made my careful way over to him, where a piece of fabric poked out of a hole which had hastily been filled in. Moving slowly so as not to slip, I caught the fabric with my hand and tugged. A small bag came free in my hand, sealed with a piece of rope.

"What on earth is in there?" Mart peered at the fabric. "Not a body, then. Unless it's a rat and not a human."

"Better not be." I removed the rope and opened the bag to reveal a pungent smell that made me cough. "You've got to be kidding me."

"*Is* it a rat?"

"No." I marched over to Drew's side and held up the bag for inspection. "Check this out."

Drew coughed. "Those smell strong."

"Yes, and we've solved the mystery of what the coven

did with the herbs needed to summon a ghost." I lowered the bag, seething. "Unbelievable."

But had they stolen Belinda's body too? What would be the point, especially if Belinda had buried the herbs herself?

"What's that?" Tessa walked over to us, raising her eyebrows at the state of my clothes.

I held up the bag and showed her the contents. "This is the coven's property. Someone took it out here to bury it."

Specifically, Belinda. Had the *coven* arranged her death? No, that didn't make any sense either. But when I'd seen her walking out of their headquarters, she must have been meeting with Marie and the others, and they'd somehow convinced her to dispose of the herbs so I wouldn't be able to summon any ghosts. Why they'd asked a non-coven member to do it, though, I had no idea.

"That's what Belinda was doing?" Tessa guessed. "Weird."

"Tell me about it." I closed the bag, since the smell was starting to make my eyes sting. "I don't think we're going to find any bodies buried out here, and besides, I have another reason to talk to the coven again."

"Exactly." Drew looked up at the sky. "It'll be dark soon, though. We should head back to town."

I definitely wouldn't be paying the chief another visit with my clothes in this state, but Tessa accompanied us back to town, true to her word. Mart floated behind us but didn't say much, not even to comment on my mud-stained appearance. Perhaps he'd realised the gravity of the situation. Let's face it, we'd be lucky to avoid the pack declaring war on one another by the day's end.

Yet it was the bag in my hands that weighed on my

mind as I struggled to form links between the coven and the pack, the killer, and the body thief. It was almost fully dark when we reached the shifters' territory, and the sound of several howls made the hairs on my arms stand on end.

"Maybe I should have waited until tomorrow." Tessa glanced around, her shoulders tensing. "If my dad is in a mood, I mean. Are you going to arrest him?"

"I hope not to," said Drew. "Rumours aside, someone clearly wants to point the blame at your family for the murders if Shana didn't take the binoculars herself."

Tessa was silent for a moment. "I don't understand anything my sister does, but I don't see her as a murderer."

"Unfortunately, I can't ignore the presence of Belinda's property in her room," said Drew. "I wouldn't be doing my job if I did."

"I know." She released a sigh. "Detective, let me speak to them alone. Maybe I can help."

"If you're sure." He came to a halt at the corner of the street. "Oh… there she is."

Tessa swore under her breath, while Shana stared at us from the other side of the road. "What are *you* doing here?"

"Shana." Tessa met her sister's stare. "I came to see the chief."

"Did you?" Shana turned her glare on Drew and me. "So now you recruited my sister against me?"

"Excuse me?" Tessa took a step forward. "Nobody recruited me. Why did you have the property of a murder victim in your room?"

"Because someone planted it there." Her voice rose in

volume. "I've had enough of being accused of murdering the man I hoped to marry."

"We never accused you of murder." I said this as much for Tessa's benefit as Shana's. "If someone *did* plant the binoculars, we need to find out who it was."

"Then why did you go and hassle my sister?"

"We went to search her property and found this." I held up the bag. "It's the coven's, and Belinda was the one who buried it."

"I don't care about the coven," she spat. "I care about the pack, and you don't belong here."

"Shana!" Tessa approached her sister, who let out an inhuman snarl. Fur began to sprout from her limbs. Oh boy.

I tensed, while Drew caught my arm. "Maura, you should leave. I'll be okay."

Across the road, the chief's two daughters growled at one another. And I thought Mart and I had a weird sibling relationship. "I know, but the chief... he can't get away with this."

"You have the means of summoning a ghost now," he said in a low voice. "If you can get her testimony, it would help."

"I'll try."

I took off at a quick stride which turned into a run when more howls rose in the background. I didn't stop running until I reached the other side of the park.

"Slow down!" Mart said. "You're leaving me in the dust."

"At least you don't lose your breath," I wheezed, slowing to a power walk. "Where should I try the summoning?"

"Anywhere that isn't in public," he responded.

"Not inside the inn either." I kept up the pace until I'd crossed to the other side of the bridge.

Once I was close to the inn, I picked a spot near the riverbank before opening the bag. It'd been a while since I'd needed to use a witch-style summoning, but I remembered the right portions of herbs to lay out in a circle on the ground. The failure rate of using regular magic to summon a ghost was much higher than the Reaper method, but it was all I had left.

With the circle complete, I stood and faced the centre. "Hey, Belinda. I need to talk to you."

Silence ensued. *Not again.*

"Belinda." I raised my voice. "Belinda, I want to talk to you."

I stood there yelling at the stupid circle for about five minutes before I noticed we'd drawn the attention of several ghosts who definitely *weren't* the one I was looking for. I carefully gathered up the herbs and put them away in the bag, figuring that the dirt wouldn't do them any harm. They'd been buried underground already, after all.

Belinda buried them for the coven. Who, then, had killed her? Had they seen to her ghost's disappearance? Or was the problem solely with my Reaper powers?

"I don't get it," I muttered to myself. "It can't be my Reaper powers affecting the spell, surely."

"Belinda must have moved on," Mart said. "If she saw the door to the afterlife, she was the sort who'd have tried to open it and run through."

"I guess," I relented. "But if she can't tell us who the killer is, will Drew be able to get a confession without the pack kicking him out and dispensing justice in their own way?"

Mart didn't have an answer for that, and nor did I.

Another nagging question remained. If I'd failed to sense Belinda's death as well as finding her ghost, could I truly call myself a Reaper at all?

"The coven did *what?*" Jia asked me the following morning.

"They had Belinda bury the missing herbs out in the field." The previous evening, I'd returned to the inn after Jia had left her shift, so I hadn't been able to give her an update on how my excursion with Drew had ended.

"You mean the ghost-summoning herbs?" A pause. "Did the *coven* steal her body, you think?"

"I don't know, but she must have been working for them after all." I should have guessed when I'd seen her exiting the witches' headquarters. "The confusing part is that we found Belinda's binoculars inside the chief's daughter's bedroom."

"The werewolf chief's daughter? Seriously?"

"Yes, and the first murder victim was her fiancé." I'd been awake half the night, trying to make all the pieces fit, but without any luck. Drew hadn't updated me on how Tessa's fight with her sister had turned out, nor whether he'd taken a team to confront the chief yet either.

"I wouldn't think the coven would want anything to do with werewolf politics," she said. "But I've been out of town for a while. I didn't think Belinda was even in the coven herself. Must be a recent development."

"Marie and her friends probably recruited her and asked her to hide the herbs, but it'd make a lot of sense for a witch to be the killer. They could have sneaked up on the victims without being detected and also slipped into the morgue through the back door and stolen Belinda's body."

"Yeah, werewolves don't really do stealth." Jia snorted.

"And the witches could have sneaked into Shana's room to plant the binoculars there," added Mart, floating out of the kitchen behind us.

"If she was telling the truth and she didn't steal them herself." I turned to Jia. "There's another dilemma to consider. It turns out the first victim bought a winning lottery ticket the day he died, and it also turns out the chief is broke."

"And the victim was meant to marry his daughter?"

"You've got it," I said. "Drew and I were on our way to speak to the chief again after we found out, but his two daughters got into a brawl and derailed us."

Her brow furrowed. "So we have two killers, potentially? Or the coven is aiding the shifters who killed Davey? What happened to the lottery money, do you know?"

"Davey's parents took it and left town," I replied. "I don't blame them. The chief was spreading rumours that their friends and allies were responsible for their son's death. All the signs point to the chief's own family being the culprits, but… I don't know."

Where did the coven fit into it? Would Drew even be able to bring the chief to justice, or would it be a repeat of the incident with Mina Devlin, and Chief Quinn would either leave town, or worse, drive out anyone who opposed him?

That depended on how much support he had among the pack, but if the person responsible for the deaths had the power of the coven on their side as well as the pack chief, it'd be even harder to challenge them.

Unless we cornered the coven members before we confronted the werewolf chief.

"Mina Devlin would have loved the drama," Jia remarked. "Poor Belinda, though. I wonder how she ended up joining the coven? I bet they bullied her into it."

"Sounds like them," I said. "When you saw her in the middle of the field the other day, what was she doing?"

"Stargazing. She claimed to be looking for the moon."

"During the day?" Was it worth assigning logic to anything she'd done? Probably not. "Never mind. I wonder how much influence the coven had over her actions. Did *she* poison Davey, and then the coven killed her in turn to cover their traces?"

"You'll have a hell of a job proving that," Mart put in. "Are you sure you want to pick a fight with the coven now that Drew isn't around to back you up?"

"What's he even doing?" I checked my phone, but I found no messages. Worry fluttered inside my chest. "I hope he didn't try to confront the chief alone."

I'd be hard-pressed to help him without my Reaper

powers, of course, but the evidence we had against the chief was flimsy at best. Compared to what we had on the coven, anyway. The bag of buried herbs was in my rucksack, and I fully intended to take it directly to them after my shift ended.

"Didn't he want you to back him up?" Jia asked.

I looked away. "No… well, the rest of the pack doesn't want me around. They think I'm a bad influence on him and that I'm turning him against the chief."

"That sounds like the shifters." She tutted. "Same with the coven. When in doubt, blame the outsider. You still want to confront the coven, though?"

"I want to know if they'll admit to anything when I show them the bag of herbs I found in the field," I explained. "It'd be easier if I could have summoned Belinda's ghost, but it didn't work."

"Didn't it?" she asked. "I guess ghost summoning isn't exactly a reliable art, unless you're a Reaper."

"Not even then." No point in hiding it any longer. "My Reaper powers have been acting up all week. I tried asking old Harold, and he implied they're wearing out."

"Is that possible?" A frown tugged on her mouth. "I thought old Harold didn't talk to anyone, aside from grouching around the graveyard and yelling at anyone who goes near him."

"He does that, but he also helped me keep the Reaper Council off my back and didn't report me for being a rogue Reaper who's operating on her own."

"Wow. You might be the first person to have stirred him into doing anything for someone else in years."

"Since the floods," I said absently. "It doesn't matter now, but it's a pain to be without my Reaper powers when

I need to confront the coven *and* the shifters. I have my wand, but I can't out-magic the entire coven."

"You might stand a chance if I'm with you."

I managed a smile. "It's appreciated."

All the same, I remained preoccupied throughout the rest of my shift, and when Mart cornered me on my way to my room to get changed, I told him to get out from under my feet. "What?"

"You're not going to have any luck with the witches if that's your attitude," he told me. "Frankly, you're making me want to dive back into my grave."

"What attitude?" I checked my phone. No word from Drew, though I'd messaged him earlier asking if he was okay. "If I'm preoccupied, it's because the werewolf pack is under the control of a potential murderer who may or may not be linked to a certain coven leader with a price on her head."

"And you think you can't stop her without your Reaper powers."

"If that was supposed to be reassuring, Mart, you missed the mark."

"It wasn't." He flew in circles around me. "Look, you haven't even tried to use your powers aside from that time at the witches' headquarters."

"You mean my shadow-walking abilities?" He had a point, but the humiliation of walking headfirst into the door twice in a row had put me off. "Do you not remember how it turned out last time?"

"I'm sure you can still do it if you aren't a drama queen about it."

"Coming from the drama king of the afterlife?"

"That is an amazing title." He twirled on the spot. "I think I'll keep it."

"You're insufferable, you are." But he'd given me an impetus. *Dammit, I will do it this time.*

Shadows flowed from my hands, covering my surroundings. I stepped forward, envisioning the doorstep, but my feet didn't budge from the floor of the reception area. I tried again, and this time I barely gripped the shadows for a few seconds before they slipped away from me.

"What am I doing wrong?" I muttered. "This is ridiculous. I could have solved all our problems if I'd just dragged the werewolf chief into the darkness for a few seconds until I scared the fight out of him."

Mart snorted. "That's probably why the police don't hire Reapers to run interrogations."

"Better than him shifting into a wolf and setting the whole pack loose on Drew." How had things gone downhill this quickly? "I can't believe they turned on him that fast. I realise they don't want *me* around, but come on."

"We want you around." Carey's voice drifted from the direction of the door. "My mum and me."

I spun around, my ears burning. Carey and her mother had entered the inn, and I'd completely failed to notice.

"We didn't mean to eavesdrop," Allie said in apologetic tones. "Is your brother there?"

"Yeah." Admittedly, I'd also been talking to myself, but it was hardly worse than walking headfirst into a wall.

"And Drew?" asked Carey.

"He's busy with the pack." Or the pack had driven him out. I couldn't deal with the uncertainty for much longer.

Reaper powers or not, I needed to help him. "Preparing to confront the werewolf chief."

I hadn't given them all the details yesterday, but Carey and Allie had the gist of the dilemma the pack had found themselves in, with an incompetent chief who might have abetted a murderer.

"Won't he need these?" Jia walked into the reception area, carrying Belinda's binoculars in her hand. "Sorry I rummaged in your bag. I was looking for the herbs."

"Oh." I reached out and took them from her. "Oops. Those are supposed to be at the police station, but I forgot to give them back to Drew after we got distracted by the fighting werewolves."

"What are those?" Carey peered at the binoculars. "Can I look?"

I didn't see the harm, so I handed the binoculars over to her. "Belinda claimed that they helped her stargaze. We found them next to her body, but they disappeared from the morgue and then showed up in Shana's—the chief's daughter's—room."

"I wonder if someone planted them there," Jia commented. "The chief sounds like a layabout and a liar, but it's almost too convenient for him to be the killer."

"The coven is involved in this too," I reminded her. "Why else would they have had Belinda bury those herbs? Except to mess with me, I mean."

"But she died." Carey looked up at me from the binoculars. "Belinda did. Right?"

"Yeah." Allie's look of concern wasn't lost on me. "I don't want to bring trouble on the inn, so if you'd rather Jia and I didn't confront the witches..."

"Oh, don't worry about it," said Allie. "I think letting

them get away with abetting a murderer would reflect worse on us in the long run."

Given the results of our driving Mina out of town, I had my doubts, but at least Allie supported me despite my long list of recent screwups. Carey too.

"You're going to confront them, then?" she asked.

"You bet," Jia answered. "I've wanted to give Mina a piece of my mind for a long time, but I can settle for doing the same to her friends."

Carey held the binoculars up to her eyes. "Whoa. I can see the sky from here."

"It's fabric," I told her. "With stars painted on it."

"No… it's a spell." She turned them over to examine the other side. "She must have made them herself."

"Do they actually work?" Jia's brow furrowed. "What do you see?"

Carey held the binoculars up to her eyes again. "The constellations. And the moon. The full moon.

"Is it the full moon tonight?" Allie asked. "Come to think of it, it might be."

"Wait, it is?" Shifters were unusually volatile at that time, and I hadn't thought to take it into account beforehand. The full moon might have played a part in their irrational behaviour, but whether they recognised it as such remained to be seen.

"Yeah." Carey handed me the binoculars back. "Belinda made these herself?"

"She did." I held them up to my eyes, but the splotchy fabric didn't look like much to me. "Said she was looking for the moon."

Jia and I exchanged the same puzzled look. Was *that* the reason? Did it matter what phase the moon was in? To the shifters, it did, but the witches wouldn't have any reason to care. Or so I thought. I'd spent enough time with Drew to know when foul play was in progress. While I didn't know what their end goal might be, I'd bet it had Mina Devlin's name written all over it.

"I'm lost," said Allie. "If you want to go and confront the coven, though, you have my full support."

"And mine," added Carey. "I can help at the restaurant while you're gone. I know you want to find the detective too."

"If you're sure." I continued upstairs to my room to change into an outfit more suitable for a potential fight and into more practical shoes in case I needed to run anywhere. I also tried to call Drew, but my message went through to voicemail instead.

Upon returning downstairs, I headed behind the bar to fetch my bag, including the herbs I needed to show the coven as proof of their meddling.

Jia waited for me by the door. "Ready to leave? Or do you want to brew up a few potions first?"

"Nah, there's no point," I said. "We need to get this done before darkness falls, because I bet that's when the shifters will come out to play."

"Good luck," Carey called to us.

Her mother echoed her words as we left the inn. We made straight for the bridge across the river, and this time, Jia and I didn't bother using a spell to hide ourselves when we approached the high street. While I'd hoped to get to the police station to check on Drew first, no fewer than four witches waited for us on the high street. Marie and her friends must have expected our visit.

Marie's eyes bulged at the sight of Jia. "*You.* Didn't you leave town?"

"I'm back," said Jia. "Still up to your old tricks, are you?"

"What are you scheming?" demanded Angela. "Another break-in?"

Oops. They must have guessed we'd searched the storeroom, though we hadn't actually taken anything. Ah well.

I dug into my bag and pulled out the sack of herbs. "Recognise this? I found it buried in a field, and according to an eyewitness, it was Belinda Jennings who buried these herbs shortly before she was murdered."

"Who, that foolish girl?" Marie scoffed. "If you ask me, she brought her fate on herself when she insisted on hanging around those animals."

Of course she was prejudiced against shifters on top of everything else.

"Brought it on herself?" Jia echoed. "You had her running around doing your dirty work, didn't you? Don't deny it."

"If we ignore how you lied to the chief of police about your lack of supplies, then there's still the question of how someone who worked for you ended up dead," I added. "And how her body went missing too."

"Missing bodies?" Angela scoffed. "What are you trying to accuse us of this time?"

Marie's face flushed. "You have nothing on us."

"We have this." I held up the sack. "And we're prepared to take it to the police if necessary."

"Is Mina involved?" Jia asked. "Has she been keeping in touch?"

"Don't be absurd," said Marie. "Mina is gone, thanks to the Reaper Witch. And we did nothing illegal."

Jia folded her arms across her chest. "You prevented Maura from summoning the ghost of a murder victim, and then the person who helped you do it ended up dead."

"We had no obligation to hand any of our supplies over to her," countered Marie. "It means nothing."

"Nice try." I reached for my wand. "We've yet to find any evidence against anyone else, but there's plenty against you."

The other witches drew their wands, while a warning voice in the back of my head told me that we were far outnumbered. On the other hand, I refused to run away.

Jia gave a flick of her wand, causing one of the witches to stagger backwards, but she recovered fast. Four wands moved in synchrony, and a deafening blast went off, sending both of us flying into the air. My back hit the ground, the breath flew from my lungs, and Jia groaned when a second spell hit both of us. My body locked up, my arms pinned to my sides. *Paralysis spell. Ow.*

Marie and the others advanced on the pair of us, but I couldn't move an inch, not even to stop her from grabbing my wand—and Jia's too. Mart yelled and swore at them, but his ghostly skills were of no use in a fight, and none of them noticed his flailing punches.

"Where should we put them?" Marie addressed the other witches.

"Mina's office will do," Angela responded.

Marie flicked her wand. Jia and I were dragged into the air and levitated into the witches' headquarters and across the lobby.

The instant Mina's office door began to close, Jia leapt up and jammed her foot in the doorway, but it stuck fast.

"You can't lock us up!" she yelled. "You don't have the authority."

"You don't have the authority to accuse us of crimes either," said Marie. "If you think that werewolf is coming to save you, you're mistaken. It's the full moon tonight. All the shifters will be moon-drunk until dawn."

I lifted my head, slower to recover from the paralysing spell. "Drew has more control than that."

The rest of the pack, though? Not so much. The witches laughed at us as the office door closed, followed by the click of a locking charm.

14

Jia and I tried all manner of ways to break the door open, but Mina Devlin had been thorough at securing her office. We were well and truly stuck, and with no wands and no backup, the odds of escape were slim. I dug in my pockets, but all I had was the bag of herbs, and they weren't much use on their own. I did have my phone, but when I pulled it out of my pocket, I found no signal available.

"Thorough, weren't they?" Jia eyed my phone. "Mina did that. She spelled the whole building so only her own landline worked."

"How did the other witches not realise how awful she was?" I remarked.

"Some of us did," said Jia. "We either left or got driven out of town. Granted, I didn't peg her as the sort who'd abet *murder*—or her followers either."

"Do you think they might be scheming to bring her back?"

That was their main goal, I was sure, and if they'd been

as committed to finding Mina as they'd been to thwarting me, then we might find ourselves in a world of trouble before we knew it.

"It wouldn't surprise me," Jia said. "The drama with the pack would be the perfect cover."

"And it's the full moon." My heart sank. Most of the police were shifters, too, and if they ended up having to spend the night dealing with werewolves fighting one another, then they wouldn't have the time to help us. Not that anyone knew we were locked in here anyway.

"How did I not see it coming sooner?" I paced around Mina's desk. "I hoped the coven might reorganise with a new leader, but they've been in limbo since she disappeared. Guess this explains why."

"This place is totally untouched." Jia indicated the neat desk and the shelves lined with books. "They left it ready for her return."

"I wonder if she left us a handy way to break out?" I tried to open the desk drawer, but even that wouldn't budge.

"I don't suppose there's anything useful in that bag of herbs?" Jia asked. "Like fire dust or explosive swamp roots?"

"I wish." I opened the bag regardless, since it contained more than just the ingredients for a summoning spell. Some of the herbs were in small containers, while others were just roots or stems bound together. The pungent smell filled the room and made it feel even more stifling.

Jia knelt beside me on the floor to examine the herbs. "What else did they want to bury, I wonder?"

"Good question." Herbalism and potions weren't my areas of expertise, though if I wanted to look up information on the herbs in the bag, a number of books filled the shelves right behind us. Out of any better ideas, I grabbed the basic textbook and flipped it open. "What do you recognise?"

"Yarrow roots and poppy seeds." She shook a small plastic container of seeds. "They're normally used in sleeping potions."

I racked my brain for the long-buried knowledge from my academy classes on brewing up potions. "Why would they try to hide them?"

"Because there's also this." She shook a jar of delicate-looking membranous wings. "Pixie wings. They're used in a potent sleeping potion so strong that it makes anyone who drinks it appear dead."

We looked at one another for a long moment. Then I shook my head. "No. Davey and Belinda are both dead. Drew or one of the other werewolves would have found a heartbeat or pulse if they weren't."

"There are ways to mask it." She rose to her feet. "I think this is it. The witches were brewing powerful sleeping potions."

"*That's* why I couldn't find Davey's ghost in the after-world. Belinda too."

But if the witches had been responsible, why hadn't they killed Davey outright? To start a war within the pack? That was plausible enough, but it didn't explain how they'd chosen their victim.

Jia began to pace the office. "I bet Belinda gave the toxin to the first victim and then took it herself. Or one of the other witches gave it to her. Either works."

"So where is she? Her body was stolen..." To prevent

the truth from getting out. What had happened to Davey, then?

"Obviously Mina's cronies didn't want to be found out," she said. "They probably threw her in a ditch somewhere."

"Sounds about right."

Where were they now? I couldn't hear anything on the other side of the door, which suggested the others had left the building altogether. Someone must have stayed behind to make sure we didn't get out, but Mart remained absent, and I didn't know if it was because he'd gone to try to warn someone or if he couldn't get into the office. The coven might have ghost-proofed the place for all I knew, but I needed to talk to Drew.

If the pack learned that Davey wasn't dead after all, then they wouldn't need to keep flinging accusations at one another. Nobody else needed to get hurt.

"If I could use my Reaper skills, I'd be able to walk through the wall and get out," I told Jia. "Too bad that's not an option."

"Hmm." She gave the door an assessing look. "Would you be able to bring another person with you?"

"If they didn't mind getting the fright of a lifetime."

A grin appeared on her mouth. "Try. It can't hurt."

Come on, Reaper skills. Cooperate with me.

Shadows appeared at my fingertips and then vanished a moment later. Jia's eyes widened. "Was that it?"

"Yeah." For the second time, shadows appeared in my hands and then vanished as though sucked into an invisible vacuum. "It keeps getting stuck."

"Are you sure something isn't blocking your powers?" she asked. "When did they start playing up?"

My mouth parted. I'd first had difficulty finding Davey's ghost… but I'd failed to sense his death or track him in the afterworld because he hadn't been dead at all. "When I tried to come into the witches' headquarters the first time."

"Did they put a booby trap on the door?"

"Yes." I'd touched the door handle and given myself a static shock. Had they mixed in some kind of spell that suppressed my Reaper skills too? If anyone was persistent enough to come up with an effective Reaper-proofing spell, it was Marie and her friends, but once I figured out how to undo what they'd done to me, I'd be able to help Drew deal with the werewolves after all.

First, though, we had to get out of here.

"Do you have any idea how to get the spell off me?" I asked Jia.

"Not without my wand," she said. "They won't leave us in here forever, though. They'll come back to gloat at some point, I guarantee."

"Then we need a plan."

An hour or two passed. By this point, it must be growing dark outside, the full moon rising in the sky. Time was running out, and with each passing second, my tension grew. I paced the room, while Jia perched on Mina's desk and watched the door.

When the sound of footsteps came from outside the room, she leapt into action. The instant the door opened, Jia barrelled into the person on the other side. I glimpsed her grappling with a red-haired witch and grabbed one of Mina's heavyweight textbooks before lobbing it at her companion, a dark-haired witch who hardly looked out of her teens. Two of them meant we were evenly matched, so I leapt through the gap in the door to join Jia, wielding another heavy textbook like a shield.

"Hey, there." Jia headbutted the first witch in the face, and she toppled into a groaning heap. "Care to tell us what you did with our wands?"

"No!" she growled.

The dark-haired witch waved her own wand, but when I flung another textbook, her spell missed wildly, bouncing off the wall.

Jia plucked a wand from the red-haired witch's pocket. "I'll borrow yours instead, then."

When she waved it, the red-haired witch went flying through the open door into Mina's office. The other witch ran to her defence, but I stuck out my foot and tripped her. She fell flat on her face, and I scooped up her wand.

Jia coaxed her into Mina's office and locked the door with a flick of the wand she'd borrowed. "Sorted. Not as good as my own wand, but I bet they left them somewhere in here."

Mart floated into the lobby. "There you are! I couldn't get into that office at all."

"Did you fetch backup?" I walked to the nearest classroom and peered inside, but I didn't see our wands. "Or pass on a warning?"

"None of the police could see me, but I thought you ought to know that Drew isn't at the office," he said. "I *did* see some of the witches heading out of town, though."

"Out of town?" Was that where Marie and Angela had gone? "You mean through shifter territory?"

"You've got it."

Jia emerged from a classroom with our two wands in her hand. "Catch."

I snagged my wand in my fingertips, while Jia waved her own wand in my direction. "What was that?"

"I'm trying to figure out what spell they used on you." She thought for a moment and flicked her wand again.

The feeling of a veil lifting in my mind washed over me, and the shadows returned to me, dark as ever.

"Whoa!" I staggered back, marvelling as the darkness washed over me. "It worked?"

"Looks that way."

Darkness folded around my feet, and a grin came to my mouth. "That's more like it."

Mart whooped. "You got your magic back?"

"The witches were behind that one too." I kept my wand in my hand as I ran for the exit, all too happy to leave the coven's headquarters behind. "Not sure what they used. Do you know, Jia?"

"Whatever it was, a generic hex removal spell took care of it."

Outside, the sky had grown dark, though I couldn't see the full moon amid the clouds yet. I crossed the road, making for the police station.

"Are you sure the police will be around?" Jia asked. "Mart, you said Drew wasn't there?"

"He'll be on shifter territory." I checked my phone for messages now that I had a signal, but not so much as a single missed call showed up. *Something happened to him.* Worry gnawed at my insides. "I think. Maybe the witches got to him first."

"Or the other way around," said Mart. "You'd have to be mad to mess with the shifters during the full moon."

"Their plan involved the moon, I'm sure. Belinda wouldn't have been fixated on it otherwise."

"You think her ramblings meant anything?" Jia arched a brow.

"Carey said those binoculars of hers actually do show the night's sky, complete with the moon's phase. Even during the day."

"They're actually good for something? Didn't see that one coming."

"I know, right?" I neared the police station and turned towards Mart before I went in. "What did you see on shifter territory? Anything which would convince the police to send in a team?"

"Aside from Drew being missing?" he said. "No, and I didn't follow the witches out of town either."

"They'd better hope they don't trespass near Tessa's house." On second thought, maybe that was exactly what they deserved. "Wait. Now I have my Reaper powers back, I can track him. Drew, I mean."

"Track him?" Jia echoed.

"My powers work like a compass," I explained. "I can find any person, if I want to. Any ghost too."

"Wow." She eyed the shadows in my hands approvingly. "I can see why you sometimes end up helping the police."

"The downside is that I can't track anyone I haven't already met, and I can't always see *where* the person is before I land next to them." If I tried to track one of the witches, for instance, I might walk straight into a trap. "I'll ask the police before I take the leap."

Inside the police station, the reception area was deserted aside from a young blond woman sitting at the front desk.

"Hey." I approached her. "I don't suppose you've seen Drew?"

She looked me up and down as if considering how much to tell me. "He went out earlier."

"How much earlier?"

"This morning."

My heart sank. "Didn't he take anyone with him?"

"Not to my knowledge."

What is he doing? I thought he was going to take a team to confront the chief. Unless the rest of the team had taken the chief's side over his.

"I think he's in trouble," I said. "I also have proof that the witches who used to belong to the coven are up to something. Marie and Angela are the ringleaders, but others are involved as well."

The receptionist's expression was almost bored. "Is that so? What proof do you have?"

I held out the bag of herbs. "The person who buried these in the field was acting on the orders of the witches in question. This contains the ingredients to make a powerful sleeping potion that makes someone appear to be dead. I believe the two recent homicides weren't deaths at all and that the witches also stole Belinda's body from the morgue in order to cover their tracks."

The receptionist continued to look unimpressed. "I can't take your word for it on that. You'll have to wait until Drew is back."

"There's no time." If he'd been missing all day, who knew where he'd ended up by now? I should have gone looking for him sooner. "Never mind."

"I think she might have taken a potion herself," Jia

murmured in my ear as we left through the automatic doors. "To counter the effects of the full moon."

"Typical." I quickened my pace, angling towards the shifters' territory. "The rest of the police must be on shifter territory. Maybe they're all running around in the fields as wolves."

"Did you say the deaths were *faked?*" Mart floated ahead of me. "Since when?"

"We found the ingredients to brew a powerful sleeping spell in the same bag as the summoning herbs," I explained. "It explains why I never sensed Davey or Belinda die and why I couldn't find their ghosts."

"They're not dead." Mart tailed me towards the park. "Why go to those lengths to fake someone's death?"

"I wonder how much Belinda knew?" Jia hurried behind me. "Was she an innocent bystander or complicit?"

"Both, maybe," I replied. "If she's the one the coven told to use the potion on Davey, she must have agreed to it."

Maybe they'd used the potion on her so she wouldn't get cold feet and give the game away, but did that mean she was on our side or against us? I didn't know, but she might be anywhere besides. Davey, too, if his body had been taken as well. It wouldn't surprise me if it had.

The sound of howling drifted from deeper in the shifters' part of town, but I didn't dare slow down. At least if things got ugly over there, I could use my Reaper powers to defend myself or escape if necessary.

"Where are you going?" Jia asked. "To see the chief? I doubt the werewolves are receiving visitors."

"It's that or track the witches using my Reaper skills and land on top of them."

"Fair point." She grimaced when howling came from closer, somewhere near the park. "Do you want to tell the wolves their friend isn't dead, then?"

"If any of them are in a fit state to listen." It might take digging up Davey's body to bring them proof, and I had the sneaking suspicion he wasn't buried at all.

Had his parents known, though? They'd left town straight after the burial, which had been kept to a limited circle of people. For all I knew, they'd known their son wasn't dead all along. Nothing would surprise me at this point.

"I wouldn't count on it," said Jia. "The witches, though… there must be quite a few of them involved. We saw four earlier and left two of them behind. It's no surprise that Marie and Angela are the ringleaders, since they were among Mina Devlin's closest friends."

"I should have made a list of her supporters, but I made it to a grand total of one coven meeting before I deposed her."

"Seriously?" Jia laughed. "Bet she never saw you coming."

"She didn't," Mart answered. "Now we're about to do the same with the werewolf chief."

"I swear I don't walk into these situations on purpose," I said sheepishly. "I just seem to aggravate them."

"Nah, I'd say most of those situations would have blown up sooner or later anyway," Jia remarked. "It's just a question of timing and whether you choose to stand your ground even if things get worse to start off with."

True. Jia had tried to defy Mina Devlin once before and had ended up being run out of town. Others had likely tried the same, and the coven had intentionally driven off anyone else who might have challenged her. Which meant there was a strong chance she had more supporters left in town than I'd previously known.

I'd have to re-evaluate my plan to ignore the former coven leader altogether, that was for sure. For now, it was her followers who were our biggest concern… tied with a pack of angry werewolves.

15

We reached the other side of the park without any of the werewolves jumping on us, at which point I headed for Davey's family's street. His parents might have left town, but if his brother was still around, he deserved to know Davey wasn't dead after all. Based on his reactions, I was reasonably confident that he hadn't been aware of the cover-up.

"You're going to see that Lewis Rogers?" Mart guessed. "I wonder how the coven picked out their victims, anyway. Davey's a weird choice."

"Maybe his family volunteered him to get out of his wedding when they found out he had that winning lottery ticket." It was as good a guess as any.

"That means they must have known the chief was broke," said Mart.

"The witches might have told them," Jia put in. "They've been meddling around shifter territory for a while, I bet."

"If we go with that theory, his parents pretended to

bury him and then left town with the money," I concluded. "I wonder if his brother was in on it?"

"Are you sure his fiancée didn't fake his death so they could secretly elope?" Jia suggested. "I don't know. I'm just throwing out ideas."

"At this point, nothing would surprise me." My pace quickened as the howling in the background grew louder. Perhaps someone in the park had spotted us after all. "If Lewis doesn't go for it, I'll try the chief."

"I'll check and see if he's hairy or not." Mart drifted away, while I reached Lewis's house and knocked.

The door opened to reveal the scowling werewolf. "You again?"

"He's not dead," I said, without preamble. "Davey isn't dead. He's been under the effects of a sleeping potion the whole time."

"Are you out of your mind?"

"No, it's true," I went on. "Someone faked Davey's death, and I think they wanted to intentionally stir up trouble in the pack. The coven is involved, and they're using the full moon as a diversion."

Howling filled the background, and Lewis's jaw tensed. "You liar."

"Wait—" I took a step back as the door slammed in my face.

As the door closed, Jia caught me up. "No luck?"

"He didn't believe me," I told her. "But if we let the chief know that Davey isn't dead after all, we might be able to stop the pack members from attacking one another."

More howls filled the air, while Mart flinched. "Ah,

Maura? I think we might be a little too late for that. The chief's not in."

"Not in?" The howling grew louder. "Has he gone out for a moonlight run?"

Was he running amok under the light of the full moon? That didn't strike me as responsible behaviour, but all bets were off on the night of the full moon, when the shifters' instincts ran wild. We wouldn't be able to count on any of them to act reasonably. I listened out, and the howls weren't coming from the park.

They were heading straight for us.

"Ah." Jia took a step back. "I don't think they want witches on their territory."

Shadows folded around my feet. At least one thing was finally functioning again. "Want me to take you with me to find Drew?"

"It's not exactly a comfortable mode of transport," said Mart. "Drew wasn't a fan."

"I'll risk it." She trod warily towards me. "Anything I need to do?"

"Hold my arm, and don't let go." I didn't think she'd end up eternally stuck in the afterworld if she did, but I'd rather not take the risk on someone who'd never been shadow-walking with me before.

Jia grabbed my sleeve, and I took a step through the shadows. I heard her inhale sharply next to me, and then I fixed an image of Drew in my mind's eye before finishing the jump.

We landed on a stretch of muddy grass, with a field stretching away to either side of us. Nearby stood several cloaked figures wearing pointed hats, waving their wands and shooting bright sparks up to the sky.

A cage sat behind them, and inside lay a werewolf. While he'd shifted into his wolf form, I recognised him even from a distance.

Drew.

Anger flared inside me, and I struggled to rein in my temper to avoid alerting the witches. They'd jumped Jia and me earlier because we'd been cocky enough to think the two of us could take on all of them at the same time. If I drew their attention, I'd lose the element of surprise, but I didn't want to give them another free minute to enact whatever plan they were brewing. Besides, caging a werewolf on the full moon was just asking for trouble.

Jia flicked her wand and rendered herself unseen, but I didn't bother with stealth. I walked straight past the witches towards Drew's cage, pointing my wand at the door. An unlocking charm caused it to spring open, but Drew didn't move an inch. Was he unconscious? Or under the effects of the same sleeping potion they'd used on Davey and Belinda? *Uh-oh.*

The witches whirled to face me, wands circling in the air, but they didn't break off whatever spell they were casting. Marie wagged a finger at me with her free hand. "You aren't supposed to be here."

I jerked my head at the cage. "Are you out of your minds? Do you *want* the shifters to tear one another to pieces?"

"It'll be entirely their own fault if they do," said Angela. "Step aside, or we'll make you wish you'd stayed locked up."

"I don't think so." I glimpsed Jia sneaking up on them, the unseen spell flickering around her, and raised my voice to draw their attention. "You set the werewolves up by making them think one of them was dead."

"He'll be grateful to us when he eventually wakes up." Marie laughed.

"You had Belinda use the potion on him, didn't you?" I went on. "Right?"

"She's not much of a witch, but she has her uses," said Marie. "She was eager enough to prove herself to us. In fact, she spent days spying on the werewolves and picking out a likely target."

"Then you used the potion on her and planted the binoculars in the house of one of the suspects," I concluded.

"Werewolves are so easy to manipulate," Angela scoffed. "We didn't even have to kill anyone. With the detective indisposed and the pack at one another's throats, nobody will challenge us, not even you."

"I beg to differ." I raised my hands, revealing the shadows beneath. "Your piece of trickery didn't work."

Marie paled. "Wait just a minute."

Jia leapt at them from behind. A spell went off like a firecracker, turning the mud beneath the witches' feet into a giant sinkhole. They slid backwards, wands flying from their hands. Marie managed to keep her balance, but an impressive amount of mud splattered her from behind. Mart laughed uproariously as the witches struggled to regain control without dropping their wands.

I grinned at Marie. "Going to tell us everything now?"

"I don't know what you mean!" she protested. "This isn't fair."

"We might be willing to give you the benefit of the doubt if you admit what spell you were casting."

As I spoke, the shadows around my feet edged towards her and the others. The witches instinctively flinched away the best they could while up to their ankles in mud.

Jia flicked her wand again, and the witches cried out as her spell hit the ground at their feet. The mud thickened, rising to cover their ankles.

"Stop that!" Angela wailed.

Jia shot me a mischievous look. "That ought to hold them."

"Nice going." I ran towards Drew's cage. He wasn't asleep or unconscious, as I thought, and his eyes opened when he saw me.

But he didn't shift back into a human. Instead, he growled at me.

"Hey, Drew. It's just me."

Another growl. I ducked when he barrelled out of the cage, still in the form of a wolf, and then ran across the field.

"Wait!" I hurried after him, but the muddy field slowed me down. He was too fast for me to keep up with even running full tilt, and he soon disappeared somewhere in the surrounding fields.

As I neared Tessa's farmhouse, she ran out of her house in shifted form, growling. Recognising me, she turned into a human again, landing barefoot in the mud. "Was that Drew?"

"Some of the ex-coven members had Drew captured in a cage." I pointed at the flailing figures trapped in the muddy field. "I don't know what they did to him, but he didn't shift back when I set him free."

"Scumbags," she said. "I saw them from a distance, but

I didn't know they caught Drew. What are they playing at?"

"They wanted to start a war among the pack," I told her. "Davey isn't dead. Neither is Belinda."

Her eyes widened. "Not dead? What... how is that possible?"

"The witches used a potion which made them appear dead," I explained. "Davey's brother wouldn't take my word as proof, but his parents knew, I think."

Her lips pressed together. "Ah... I think I know where his parents went, and if he's alive, then they'll have taken him with them."

"I can't be in two places at once." I scanned the area for any signs of Drew's wolf form, but he'd vanished from sight. "I need to find Drew and tell the other werewolves that Davey isn't dead."

"And... Belinda." She hesitated. "I have her. In my house. I found her body lying near my property and worried she'd get eaten by wildlife, so I brought her indoors. I was going to return her to the morgue, but I didn't know how to avoid getting blamed for stealing her body to begin with."

"You have her?" Belinda's body had been inside her house all along?

She gave me a sheepish look. "I know I look guilty, but she really does seem to be dead. I didn't want to go to jail for murder or body snatching."

"Fair enough. The witches probably wanted you to get blamed."

I'd bet they'd wanted to get *me* out of the way, too, but I'd thrown a wrench in their plans.

Tessa drew in a breath. "I can find Davey's parents and

ask them to give him back, but I have no idea how to wake him up."

"That's the witches' job," I said. "I'm sure I can convince them to tell me how to counter the potion they used."

"Then I'll be back before you know it." She broke into a run, shifting into her wolf form, while I returned to the field where Jia supervised the trapped witches.

"Who was that?" Jia indicated Tessa's retreating wolf form. "Do the wolves out here just walk around in the mud without any clothes on all the time?"

"Pretty much," I said. "It turns out Belinda's body is hidden in Tessa's farmhouse because she found her lying around in a field, but she's gone to find our elusive, missing would-be groom. I guess it's up to me to stop the pack from murdering one another until she comes back."

"What do you want me to do with them?" She indicated the witches. "I think they're more secure here than in the jail if the majority of the town's police team is running around with the wolves."

"Maybe, but I need to find Drew before I can talk to the rest of the pack," I said. "They won't believe me unless he backs me up."

"You can't leave us in here!" Marie yelled from the mud.

"Yes, we can," said Mart. "Also, your boyfriend went over there, Maura, but he's still all hairy and growly. I don't think he wants to be disturbed."

"Too bad." I followed his line of sight, but I didn't need to be able to see Drew in order to track him down.

"You'll pay for this," Angela spat from behind me.

"Says who?" Jia retaliated. "Mina Devlin? Was that

whose attention you were trying to draw with that fancy spell of yours? You'd better hope she *doesn't* come back while you're stuck in here, because she has a nice cosy cell waiting for her."

She did, but only Drew could put her in there. If I was willing to throw myself in his path while he was out of control under the light of the full moon, of course.

I concentrated on his image in my mind's eye, and then I stepped through the shadows and landed in a patch of grass under a large tree. Drew's wolf form prowled at its base, and he spotted me before the shadows faded away. A faint snarl slipped between his teeth.

"What's with you?" My heart thundered against my ribcage. "You haven't forgotten how to turn back into a human, have you?"

The witches might have put a spell on him, but the moon itself might as easily be the culprit. In any case, when he growled at me again, I reached out and grabbed his furry paw. Then I pulled him into the shadows along with me.

As I'd hoped, he didn't attack me—the afterworld was a scary place, even to a werewolf—but I hadn't mentally prepared myself for the sight of his naked human form appearing in his place when we landed in the field again.

He looked blearily at me. "Maura?"

"Sorry." I tried to keep my eyes on his face. I really did. "I didn't know how else to shock you into shifting back."

"It worked," he said. "And you… you saved me."

"With help." I sucked in a breath. "Drew, Davey isn't dead, but he's under the effects of a powerful sleeping potion. Tessa has gone to find him, but we need to stop the pack from killing one another before she comes back. Also, why didn't you mention today was the full moon?"

Tessa had already vanished into the distance, and I hoped she'd be able to find Davey and his parents' hiding place in time to prevent any more chaos. I couldn't believe they'd gone to such lengths to get out of the wedding, but then again, the witches had been stoking the shifters' rage for weeks. All it'd needed was a spark to set off the fire… and that spark in question had been the full moon.

As for stopping the pack from attacking one another? That was Drew's job, not mine.

"He's alive?" His eyes widened. "And Belinda?"

"She's unconscious in Tessa's farmhouse," I replied. "Would it help our case if we took her back to the others to prove she isn't dead?"

"Not if we can't wake her up." He shifted into a wolf and ran towards the farmhouse, forcing me to jog in order to keep up with him.

"It was the witches," I told him. "They might have the antidote with them, or they might have left it at their base."

He veered away from the farmhouse and towards the struggling witches, but I didn't stop until I reached the farmhouse.

"She's in there." Mart indicated a small shed at the side of the farmhouse. "Good job the chief didn't search the property the other day."

"Tell me about it." The door was easy to open with a wave of my wand, and I found Belinda lying on the floor, looking so still and quiet that I would have believed her dead if I hadn't known otherwise. "Guess I'll have to carry her back."

"Or your boyfriend can, but he seems to have done a runner."

Not again. "Maybe he's putting some clothes on."

"Bet you'd prefer it if he didn't."

I opted not to dignify that with a response, instead hauling Belinda's body over my shoulder. Her dead weight was heavier than I'd expected, and I nearly dropped her when Drew growled at me from outside the farmhouse.

"Not again." I adjusted my grip on Belinda. "If you're going to stay like that, then you'll have to give me some kind of signal so I can understand you. Want me to take you through the shadows back to shifter territory?"

He dipped his head, saying yes.

"I can't say I've ever tried this with an unconscious person as well as a werewolf, but there's a first time for everything."

"I'd help, but you know." Mart waved his transparent hands. "It might interest you to know the howls are coming from the park."

"That's where the chief is." My shoulders ached from carrying Belinda already, so I nodded to Drew. "Put a paw on my leg so I don't lose you."

He did so, his paw surprisingly soft, and Mart snickered under his breath. "If you ask me, he's worried that shifting back into a human will give more away than he intended to."

I'd have made a rude gesture if I had either of my hands free, but I had to settle for a glower. "See you on the other side."

Then, with Belinda's body in my arms and Drew at my side, I stepped into the shadows.

Grass appeared beneath my feet, and I staggered, Belinda's body slipping from my grip. Drew let go of me, and I raised my head to see the deep greenery of the park —and two groups of werewolves squaring up to one another.

Oh boy. It looked like we'd got here just in time.

Everyone turned towards Drew, and my blood chilled to hear their growls and snarls. He growled straight back at them, while I gestured towards Belinda's body.

"Stop fighting!" I shouted. "Belinda's alive, and so is Davey."

Drew ran towards them, while I followed close behind, holding my shadows like a protective shield in case any of them jumped at me. I could only assume that Drew was explaining everything to them in werewolf-speak, because I couldn't understand a word amid the growling.

A bright light flashed somewhere behind us, but before I could glance over my shoulder to find the cause, Lewis Rogers shifted into human form. "My brother is dead. You're lying."

"I'm not." I spoke loudly enough for the rest of the pack to hear me too. "Your parents made a deal with the coven to fake his death so that they didn't have to share his winning lottery ticket with the chief. The coven was already on the lookout for a werewolf whose death they wanted to fake in order to provoke the pack into a war, and Belinda Jennings found them the perfect candidate."

"What kind of nonsense is that?" Shana shifted into human form next, her teeth bared. "You dare to use my fiancé to back up your lies? Was accusing my family of murder not enough for you?"

Behind her, a loud growl rose from one of the largest werewolves. The chief.

"Listen to me." I addressed the werewolves as a collective. "The witches were manipulating you into fighting with one another on the full moon on purpose. They captured Drew, and they were in the middle of casting a spell to draw back their disgraced coven leader, Mina Devlin, when I managed to stop them. If you want me to show you proof, they're trapped in the field near Tessa's house."

"Her!" Shana exploded. "My sister had the nerve to show up at my house yesterday and treat me like dirt after ignoring me for months, and now she's helping you conspire against my family."

"Tessa has gone to find Davey and his parents and bring them back to town." I ignored her outburst and continued to speak to the rest of the pack. "And Belinda…"

"I'm here." Belinda herself was back on her feet, not at all like she'd been unconscious less than five minutes prior. "Has anyone seen my binoculars?"

Nobody moved. She seemed entirely oblivious to the number of angry werewolves surrounding her, but most of them looked too stunned to attack.

"She was dead," said Lewis slowly.

Another werewolf shifted back too. "She's been alive the whole time?"

"I told you." I directed that part at Lewis then turned to Belinda. "How did you wake up?"

Jia appeared from the nearby bushes, holding up a bottle so that we could all see. "I snagged the antidote from the witches. They aren't going anywhere, so I figured I could leave them for a minute to bring this."

She must have used a transportation spell to jump here, which explained the bright flash I'd seen a couple of minutes ago. "Good timing."

"Tessa is fetching Davey," I added to the other werewolves, several of whom had joined their companions in shifting back into human form. "He'll be ready to wake up, too, once we can give him the antidote. His parents knew about this. The coven persuaded them to help—"

"By faking his death?" Lewis finished. "No. My brother wouldn't—he wanted to marry Shana. I think he was the only one who actually *wanted* the wedding to go ahead."

"What?" Shana squeaked. "I wanted to marry him. He couldn't… he can't have been alive the whole time."

The pack broke into noise, growls and questions rising into a cacophony. The chief brought the arguments to a brief halt by barking out an order—literally. Then he shifted into a human and glowered at me. "Look at what you've brought upon us, human."

Typical of him to fling the blame at me. He stood in the middle of the pack without a stitch of clothing. I was glad of the darkness to spare me from that mentally scarring sight, that was for sure.

"You should be glad the coven's attempts to frame your family for their deaths didn't work," I told him. "I bet they broke into your house, too, when they planted the binoculars in Shana's room."

That didn't change the fact that his money woes were right in the open now, nor that Drew had good reason to reprimand him for lying to the police *and* his entire pack.

The chief shifted into a wolf again and began barking

orders, while I found myself shoved to the sidelines next to Belinda.

"Why did the witches put *you* to sleep?" I asked. "To stop you telling tales?"

She ignored my question. "Have you seen my binoculars?"

"I'll give them back if you tell me the truth," I said. "Did you help the coven willingly?"

She gave me a bewildered look. "What do you mean?"

"They asked you to help them, right?"

"I saw this coming, you know. I saw them on the full moon."

I frowned. "You mean you saw the future?"

Jia nudged me from my other side and whispered, "Don't bother. You'll only give yourself a headache if you try to figure her out. It's up to the police to find out if she's guilty or not."

"Assuming Drew ever escapes the pack."

While I appreciated that they were no longer at one another's throats, I did wish they'd finish dealing with their squabbles so I had my own werewolf all to myself.

Several minutes passed before Drew approached me again, back in human form and wearing a pair of loose jogging trousers he must have grabbed from somewhere. "Are you okay?"

"Yeah." I indicated Belinda. "I'm not sure if she counts as a willing participant, but the other witches are already secured. You might want to send someone to fetch them."

"On it," he said. "I'll go and meet Davey before he reaches town, so his parents don't have to deal with the chief themselves."

"What's going to happen to him?" I asked. "I know he

didn't turn out to be a murderer or even complicit in the witches' crimes, but he did lie to you. And he tried to kick you out of the pack."

"I know." His expression shadowed. "The pack might need a change in leadership, but that's an issue to be resolved another day. Whatever the case, though, you're welcome among us, Maura. I can promise you that."

I smiled.

Drew might have given me his blessing on behalf of the pack, but I was kind of glad not to be around to witness the incredibly awkward aftermath of Davey's parents' return to town and his subsequent revival from *death*.

They'd opted to wait until after the full moon was over to actually meet with the chief, which was probably for the best. No doubt he'd been deeply offended that they'd gone to such lengths to get out of their son marrying Shana, even if it'd been the witches who'd convinced them to go ahead with it in the first place.

I had an inkling Shana and Davey wouldn't be picking up their engagement, though that was probably for the best for everyone involved. While Shana herself had suffered a horrible shock, I had trouble sympathising with her, considering the way she'd treated Drew and me. She and her family might have been acting under the influence of the full moon, but that didn't mean I had to go out of my way to forgive her.

Luckily for everyone, the full moon departed without the werewolves getting into another pack fight, affording Drew and the rest of the police the time to give Marie and the others hefty charges for attacking Jia and me, manipulating the shifters, and sneakily putting a spell on me to sabotage my Reaper powers. Among other things. Since they hadn't actually killed anyone and Mina Devlin hadn't shown her face, though, the punishment was more lenient than I'd have liked.

"I guarantee she saw their signal," Jia remarked to me as we stood behind the bar during a lull in our shift. "I also think they'll try the same again as soon as they're free."

"Yeah, that's what I'm afraid of." We hadn't seen the last of the witches' shenanigans, that was for certain. "If Mina does show her face, she has a price on her head. She's being careful, I'm sure."

Jia made an irritated noise. "If she's in the area, I bet we could catch her in the act if we had enough backup."

"How much is enough backup when it comes to a powerful witch who possibly still has most of the coven behind her?" I queried. "Don't get me wrong, I'd love to see Drew put her away, but it was naive of me to think her supporters weren't still acting as though she was in charge."

"I should have seen it coming too." Her lips pursed. "I might not have moved back here if I'd known she was still influencing everyone."

My mouth went dry. "Does that mean you aren't staying?"

"No, I made a promise to Allie," she said. "Besides, I'm not resisting the coven alone this time around."

"No." A heartbeat passed. "For the record, I'd prefer not to wait for her to jump us from behind before we catch her."

"Precisely my thinking too."

It wouldn't be easy to bring her in, I had little doubt. I'd need the full extent of my Reaper powers to do so, and there were Carey and her mother to consider too. I wouldn't put them in danger unnecessarily if I could help it.

"How many people do you know who left the coven?" I asked.

Jia gave me a quizzical look. "A few, but I didn't keep a list. Why?"

"I know you said you didn't suspect she was covering up murders, but might anyone else who left the coven have suspected before I did?"

"No idea," she said. "I didn't know myself until Allie explained it to me over the phone when she offered me the job."

"None of us knew either," I said. "The thing is, it's not the only time Mina's name has come up in connection with covering up serious crimes. We had to arrest a librarian not long ago for using illegal magic in an attempt to drive me out of town so I'd stop poking my nose into the coven's past misdeeds."

"Who, Debora Lowe?" she asked. "She tried to drive you off?"

"Because I can talk to ghosts, and Mina doesn't want me to hear what they have to say." I scanned the restaurant, trying not to lose my nerve. "I think we've only scratched the surface of what she's been involved in. In fact, I wonder how she got her position to begin with."

Jia shrugged. "I wish I knew. She's run the coven since before I was born."

Since before the floods. None of the ghosts I'd spoken to had any real memories of the floods, even the ones who'd met their deaths on that fateful day. I had to wonder why that was the case and what exactly the coven had been doing that day. With Mina gone and her conspirators jailed, the opportunity to speak to actual witnesses might be hard to come by. Jia was around my age, so she wouldn't remember the floods herself.

"Do you think it's worth looking into?" I pressed. "It'll be dangerous, I'll admit it. All it took was a few questions before Debora used illegal magic to summon deadly monsters from the afterworld to attack me. The rest of the coven might have worse up their sleeves."

She gave me an assessing look. "Deadly monsters, you say?"

"When you have long-buried secrets, the last thing you need to have around is a Reaper. We tend to be good at digging."

A grin appeared on her mouth. "Bring it on, then."

"Mina had total control over the town's press from the moment she took leadership," I added. "For that reason, I bet we'll have trouble finding official sources which contain any incriminating information."

"I figured," said Jia. "I'll look for the contact details of some of the witches I know of who left town, and I'll see what I can find out."

"Perfect. We need as much proof as possible. It wouldn't hurt if we convinced some of them to move back here like you did, to help squash the coven's influence on the other witches."

"That'll take some persuasion," she commented. "The town's seen better days. There aren't a ton of opportunities here."

"There will be when we set up our ghost tours at the inn." I'd been seriously neglecting helping Carey with preparations in the past week, but it'd be far easier to make progress without a potential war within the werewolf pack on the horizon.

"Anything I can do to help with that?"

"I was going to start putting out word among the local ghosts that we're looking for spirits who'd be happy to entertain our guests. Mart was supposed to be helping, but he's being stubborn."

He seemed to be enjoying his new position in the kitchen, though, and Jia's ability to see ghosts herself meant I wouldn't have to do all the recruiting alone.

"I'll see if I can convince him." She went into the kitchen, while I returned to cleaning the bar. My mood had brightened considerably. It wouldn't be easy to undo the damage Mina had done, but if we put our heads together, we'd be able to unearth the rest of her secrets.

Once we had proof, then others might come forward to back us up. Who knew, maybe even Harold the Reaper would speak up on behalf of his apprentice who'd lost his life in the floods. Granted, he seemed content to let the world pass him by, and I was still mildly irritated with him for his reaction during my last visit. If he'd actually bothered to take a look at me rather than insulting me from the other side of the door, he might have seen that I had a spell on me which blocked my Reaper powers.

The restaurant's door opened, signalling Carey's return from school. She bounded over to the bar, a grin on her mouth. "Hey, Maura. Everyone at school was talking about you."

"About *me?*"

"How you stopped a war within the werewolf pack."

"Hey, it wasn't just me," I protested. "Drew did most of the work. And Jia helped restrain Marie and her friends."

Jia emerged from the kitchen with Mart in tow. "It was a team effort."

"Yes, it was," Mart said. "Have you been slacking off all this time?"

"It's pretty quiet at the moment," I told him. "We were talking about ghost tours and how we're going to give the town a massive tourism boost so the other witches who left the coven will want to come back."

Carey's eyes brightened. "That's a good idea."

"I'll help with the ghost recruitment," Jia added. "What kind of spirits are you looking for?"

As Carey launched into an explanation, Mart beckoned towards me. Frowning, I walked after him into the inn's reception area. "What is it?"

"Don't you want to know how the witches came up with a spell that could turn off your powers?"

"Yes." It hadn't been hard for Jia to counter the spell once she'd known it existed, but the fact that they'd come up with anything at all was worrisome. "I need to look into that."

It'd certainly stall my plans to expose the coven's crimes if they managed to cut off my main advantage again. I definitely needed to do some research to find out where they'd come up with magic like that.

"You do," Mart agreed. "I'm glad it wasn't permanent. I prefer you like this, not all mopey."

"Thanks, I think," I replied. "Have you seen old Harold?"

"Nope. Should I go and poke him?"

"He might be interested to know the witches can shut off his Reaper skills." Not that he ever used them, and he rarely lifted a finger to help me anyway.

Regardless, if we did end up going against Mina Devlin again, he might be pushed to take a side next time. He ought to, really. His apprentice had died in the floods, after all.

"True." Mart's gaze went past me to the restaurant doors. "Ooh, look who it is. Pity he's wearing clothes this time."

I spun on my heel, seeing Drew enter the restaurant. "Behave, Mart. I'll be back in a second."

He laughed at my back as I walked over to meet Drew, my heart swooping when he smiled at me.

"Hey, Drew."

"Hey. Sorry I haven't dropped by. It's been a busy few days."

"I bet. Is the pack back to normal?"

"More or less," he said. "Davey and his parents decided to leave town again, this time without Davey pretending to be dead. I'm not sure they're coming back."

"Poor Shana," I remarked. "The chief is still in charge, then?"

"For now, but his reputation took a hit. I believe there'll be a vote on a new leader soon, so it depends on whether he can redeem himself before then."

"I'm not holding out much hope." That whole family was a mess, frankly, and Tessa had the right idea when she'd opted to live in the middle of nowhere. "I'm glad

Davey and his family got closure, even if I do have to wonder how Belinda managed to use a potion on him without being spotted. Did she end up being jailed?"

"No," he said. "By her own account, the other witches pressured her into helping them and then turned against her. It's lucky for her that Tessa found Belinda's sleeping body when she did."

"Is she still claiming she saw this coming?"

"Yes." His brow furrowed. "I don't tend to believe Seers, but I have to wonder if she might have picked up on their intentions. The witches kept her working in ignorance of their true motives, but I think she made the decision to hide the potion ingredients herself."

"Huh." I turned this over in my mind. "I guess she comes across as more of a victim than a perpetrator, but you might want to keep an eye on her in case one of Mina Devlin's supporters tries to recruit her again. She's a walking target."

"I did send people to look out for Mina, but she never showed up."

"Her supporters probably got her attention with that stunt they pulled, but she must have realised it went wrong," I said. "She'll be cautious, but it's safe to say she's watching for our next move."

"No doubt. We're keeping an eye out for potential trouble, but she's a sneaky one."

"I know." I lowered my voice. "Jia is going to try to contact any other witches Mina drove out of town. If we can find more proof of her crimes, it'll help, because I can guarantee we haven't seen the last of her."

His eyes flickered with something predatory that reminded me of the wolf he shifted into. "I can't arrest someone who isn't anywhere to be found, but I look forward to seeing her again."

"Same here. It might not happen for a while, but Marie and the others will only be in jail for a few years, and Mina's playing a long game. I think we have to consider the possibility that the coven won't accept another leader until she returns."

"The coven is disbanded." A growl entered his voice. "I gave all the witches strict orders not to lie to me again, and their storeroom is once again open to anyone who needs it."

"Good."

He looked around the restaurant, his gaze travelling over the bar, where Jia and Carey were engaged in an animated conversation about ghost tours. "I have to head back to the station now, but are you free this evening?"

"You want to finish our date?" A smile paused on the edge of my mouth. "Are you sure the other shifters will appreciate me visiting their part of town?"

"I'm sure most of them will," he said. "The full moon is over now. No more high tempers. Honestly, this sort of thing tends to happen a lot. I've had shifters fight me on the slightest whim and then beg for forgiveness by morning."

"Do they normally declare war on one another, though?"

"Well, no, but they're grateful for you stopping them."

"I'll have to take your word for it on that." All the same, the time was ripe for a fresh start. "Sure, then. It's a date."

ABOUT THE AUTHOR

Elle Adams lives in the middle of England, where she spends most of her time reading an ever-growing mountain of books, planning her next adventure, or writing. Elle's books are humorous mysteries with a paranormal twist, packed with magical mayhem.

She also writes urban and contemporary fantasy novels as Emma L. Adams.

Visit http://www.elleadamsauthor.com/ to find out more about Elle's books.

www.ingramcontent.com/pod-product-compliance
Lightning Source LLC
Chambersburg PA
CBHW020808190726
48285CB00006B/2207